# The Cadaver
# and
# The Shark

**George Roding**

Design & typesetting by Clare McCabe www.purplestardesign.co.uk

ISBN13:   978-1-0369-2059-3

**DISCLAIMER**

*For Marianne*
*My inspiration for this book*

# Contents

# Prologue

*Oh, the shark, babe, has such teeth, dear*
*And it shows them pearly white.*
Mack The Knife

Everything about the room was huge. The oak-beamed ceiling was high. Its length and breadth were the size of a small ballroom, and the fireplace, in front of which the two men were sitting, was big enough to walk in. Or it would have been were it not for the fact that it was filled with large gas-fuelled flames, bringing to mind the burn off from an oilfield. The flames were streaking upwards from an artificial log effect fire.

In keeping with the dimensions of the room, each of the men was engulfed by a large leather armchair with a side table on which were sitting drinks and, in one case, an ashtray big enough to accommodate a 'Cuban' cigar imported from the Dominican Republic.

Even for men of such wealth and influence, it was not the done thing to be found breaking government embargos on the import of cigars made in Cuba to the United States. Not only that, it was unpatriotic, a point which mattered to the occupant of the armchair who sincerely believed he was a greater patriot than Uncle Sam himself. In any case, good cigars were readily available since amongst the many Cubans who had left their country with the coming of Castro were cigar manufacturers who had set up shop elsewhere, particularly in the Dominican Republic, where conditions were favourable.

The man on the left of the fire had no cigar, whilst the drink on his side table was of a strangely pinkish colour, it being a specially concocted mixture of vitamins and juices designed for health rather than pleasure. Albin Millard was a frail specimen of an advanced age. His skin was pale, almost white, and underneath his domed head, a pronounced bone structure and sunken cheeks had earned him the irreverent nickname of the 'Cadaver' from staff and rivals when out of earshot. More flatteringly, he had also acquired the soubriquet 'The Wizard of Wall Street' for his investment prowess, which had made him one of the ten wealthiest men in the world and earned him a following of thousands of small investors all over America.

Opposite him sat a man cut from a very different piece of timber. Jim Doors was now in his sixties, but at six foot four, the broad-shouldered Texan still made an imposing figure. The remains of what had once been a blonde curly thatch just about covered his head, but his tanned complexion was in marked contrast to the man opposite. However, his most noteworthy physical feature only became apparent when he smiled or grinned. Above his pronounced jawline, he had the most remarkable set of white teeth imaginable. It was never clear whether this feature or his rapacious appetite for gobbling up smaller competitors was what led him to be dubbed

'The Shark'. Either way, he had built up a business empire which had recently propelled him into that exclusive club of billionaires, the richest men in the world.

Jim's first fortune had been made in boots and shoes, and he never forgot this. But it was moving into property which had promoted him to the major league. His empire now covered the country, and there were few state capitals which did not boast a tower block owned by him.

He took a sip of the copper coloured liquid in his glass, which, in contrast to the cadaver's health potion, was a twelve-year-old bourbon made exclusively for him by a small Kentucky distillery he had invested in some twenty years ago. Leaning forward, his broad grin exposed the immaculate and somewhat fearsome rows of teeth.

"Al, ol' boy, you were so right, and I have taken your advice."

The Cadaver hated it when his name, Albin, was shortened to Al, but given the company and the circumstances, he decided to let it pass. Instead, he allowed his thin lips to form the thinnest of smiles, but he said nothing and waited for the other man to continue.

"We've set up the foundation, called it The Doorstep Foundation. Neat huh? I never forget my roots."
The thin lips smiled again, but this time responded.

"Very neat".

"We're putting thirty in to start." The Cadaver nodded. They were talking billions. "My people tell me that the tax saving alone will run to more zeroes than I can count. Yes sir, philanthropy is going to be good for me!" The teeth reappeared with a broad grin. "Maddie and I will be directors, and we should be honoured if you would join us on the Board." The other man nodded, and the thin smile returned.

The Texan relaxed in his chair and took another sip of bourbon. "Let me tell you what we have planned".

Albin Millard listened intently and raised his eyebrows more than once as the Shark outlined his ambitious and audacious project. "I can see how the others will come in, but what makes you think their President will go along with this?"

"Their President? Why should we worry about their President?"

"Isn't he the man who runs the goddam country?"

The grin returned, and the teeth positively glowed in the reflected light from the flames of the fire.

# Chapter 1 - Harley Street, London

Tuesday 16 May 2017

Dr Robson Ford leant back in his chair and stretched out his long legs in front of him. He hooked his right foot around one of the patients' chairs and drew it towards him so that he could then use it as a footstall on which both of his legs could rest. Mary would disapprove, but Mary was out on her lunch break, so he would be spared the sharp Scottish tones of her reprimand. 'Patients have to sit on those chairs. I would have expected better from a senior medical practitioner'. Instead of guilt, he was always secretly amused by her prim scolding, but he dared not let that show. It wouldn't do to upset Mary, so he always took his medicine like a dutiful patient.

She was his practice nurse, administrator, and general PA, all rolled into one and came with him when he set up his private practice in Harley Street from the hospital where they had worked together. They were both glad to escape the constant reorganisations of the NHS and the pressures and chaos which such 'restructurings' usually brought about.

However, today, Dr Ford was not relaxed. There was no inward smile but rather the serious expression of a man whose mind had been disturbed. What had disturbed him had been his patient that morning.

A ten-year-old boy had presented with all the symptoms of tuberculosis, a disease which was both contagious and potentially life threatening if not treated. A quick phone call to a senior contact at his former stamping ground, the HTD or Hospital for Tropical Diseases, had resulted in young Julian Fellowes being whisked off with his mother for a series of tests, including chest X-rays, blood tests, skin tests, and possibly others to follow.

The boy's recent history was unusual, to say the least. He had only just returned with his mother from a month's stay in the small African republic of Kwandia, where his father was acting as mission administrator for a major charity with several active projects in the country. Kwandia was known to have one of the highest rates of tuberculosis not only in Africa but anywhere in the world. Another charity, with the help of foreign aid partly directed through the local Kwandian government, had embarked upon a major vaccination initiative against the disease. Julian had arrived in the country right at the beginning of this project, and when the medical caravan came to the small township where they were staying, he had lined up with the locals to receive the vaccine.

Three weeks later, he had begun to feel unwell, but not only that, many of the local inhabitants had also fallen sick, and before he had left the country, there were reports of two deaths in the town. His mother had called an abrupt halt to their planned stay of two months and rushed home with her son for treatment in London. The private medical insurance provided by her husband's employers covered all the family, so they were able to secure an early appointment with a recommended Harley Street specialist in tropical and infectious diseases.

He was confident that the boy could be treated, but there were circumstances surrounding this case which gave rise to his unease both from a medical point of view and from his own unique personal history. Medically, Dr Ford knew that further tests may be needed before he could be sure of his diagnosis. Tuberculosis was described by some as 'The Great Imitator' because it had the ability to mimic the symptoms of other diseases, and this was a distinct possibility when the circumstances were unusual. In this case, the circumstances were very unusual. Firstly, the only proven vaccine against tuberculosis he knew of was the Bacillus Calmette-Guerin vaccine or the BCG vaccine for short. This vaccine worked best with young people and was not considered effective for those over 35 years of age. Nevertheless, from what he had been told, the vaccine had been administered to every man, woman and child in the township. Whilst no vaccine is ever 100 per cent effective, he had never heard of a vaccination programme causing the very infection it was supposed to prevent on such a scale.

He was a man of whom it could be said owed his very life to a vaccine, and the thought of such a procedure giving rise to infection and death filled him with horror.

Dr Robson Ford had been born Robson Mulenga in a small village in the heart of Zambia. As he relaxed in his chair, his mind drifted back to that village and a boy not much older than Julian Fellowes. It was a hot afternoon as usual when his mother collected him from the village school and they walked four miles to a larger village where 'Dr Fiesta' had set up his clinic and was vaccinating the local children against the dreaded polio, a disease which had crippled and finally killed his elder brother. His mother was determined that the same fate would not befall young Robson, 'the brightest child in the whole of Africa' and the apple of his mother's eye.

Nobody knew the doctor's real name, but he drove his battered old Ford Fiesta on the baked mud African roads, touring the villages on behalf of a medical charity. Somehow, Dr. Fiesta was the name that stuck with the local population. In any case, it seemed to suit his cheerful, outgoing personality, and his visits were occasions to be celebrated by the local community. Robson often wondered how much this man had influenced his own choice of career, although there had been other factors at play.

From the village school, young Robson had won a scholarship to an international school in Lusaka and from there to University where he had studied medicine. In Lusaka, he had lived with the family of a distant relative with only the occasional trip home to see his mother. His formative years had, therefore, developed in him independence and maturity, which, coupled with his innate intelligence, marked him out from his peers. It was no surprise to his tutors when, upon graduation, he was offered a government-sponsored bursary to follow a post-graduate degree course in medicine at Cambridge University in England. It was also no surprise when he jumped at the chance and accepted with alacrity.

He knew it would change his life, but he could never have guessed by just how much. Of course, the quality of teaching and the knowledge he acquired elevated his professional status and his ambitions into a different league. But what really transformed his world was Alice. Beautiful, radiant Alice with her fair hair, blue eyes and trim figure was the archetypal English rose. She was studying medieval history. What else for the daughter of a career diplomat and an outlying member of one of England's oldest aristocratic families? So much had they enjoyed each other's company that it was some time before he realised that she had stopped seeing any of the other male friends who were always forming a queue to take her out and that he was her chosen one.

It was at this time that another momentous event was about to take place in his life. His course was ending, and he had begun to apply for hospital appointments. Despite his first-class academic qualifications, he was experiencing disinterest or rejection. It was Alice's idea. "We have to face it, Rob. In this country, you will always face prejudice at the outset, but we need to get you over the first hurdle. You need to get in front of them so they can see just how good you are. Why don't we change your name?"

He thought she was joking, but she persisted and began to fire off names which sounded English and she thought might suit him. He did not like the sound of any of them. Then he told her the story of Dr Fiesta back in his village. She let out a shriek of laughter "Fiesta! We can't use that. It sounds even less English than your real name." It was his turn to grin, and he drew her close to him "Idiot, don't you know that the Fiesta is a Ford. What about that for a good, solid English name?"

And so, Dr Robson Ford was born. He remembered that conversation as though it were yesterday. And he also remembered the sequence of events which followed. The visit to her parents in their Sussex farmhouse. 'Just a few acres' is how Daddy described it. In truth, it was a mixed arable and sheep farm comprising a reasonable portion of the Sussex Downs. Alice, being Alice, had not prepared her parents for the shock they were to receive. "What is his name, darling?"

"Robson"

Her mother smiled. "Oh, Doctor Robson. That sounds nice. A doctor in the family would be a great idea. None of us is getting any younger"
No, Robson is his first name. He is Doctor Ford,

and he was considered the brightest of his year at Cambridge."

It was some years later when Alice had told him of this conversation, and it only served to increase his admiration for her parents. Whatever they were expecting when they finally met him, he was pretty sure it would not have been a six-foot-three African. It was a tribute to his future father-in-law's diplomatic training that he exhibited not even the faintest hint of surprise at their first meeting, and his dutiful wife simply followed the English tradition of offering tea as if they were entertaining the local vicar. What they felt privately had never been revealed.

The wedding to Alice was a relatively low-key affair for a family who were members of the 'county' set and might have expected a more lavish and public celebration befitting a local aristocrat's daughter. In truth, the more modest event attended by family and a few genuine friends suited both of them much more and indeed proved to be a very happy occasion.

He was now the father of twin daughters, and he allowed himself a satisfied smile as he thought of them. He was also satisfied with his life as a Harley Street specialist, but he was always a realist and knew that while his own skills had earned him the right, Alice's money had funded the prestigious location and the self-employed status that accompanied it.

His daydreaming reverie was suddenly disturbed by the sound of Mary returning in the outside office, which also served as a reception area. It was time to refocus on the case of young Julian Fellowes.

# Chapter 2 - The Doorstep Foundation

He was not surprised to learn that the boy had been admitted to a private ward at the hospital. However, it was not until the following morning that all the test results were available. This was much quicker than the NHS standard, but he felt no guilt at using money and contacts to obtain an advantage. After all, he had first-hand experience of poverty and deprivation and did not wish to return there.

The tests confirmed that the boy had contracted tuberculosis. The prognosis for full recovery under hospital care was good, and he was pleased to be able to contact his mother with this news.

Nevertheless, he remained troubled by how Julian had apparently caught the disease from the vaccination and had a number of questions for Mrs Fellowes. His call to her provided more questions than answers, but he obtained some information, which gave him somewhere to start. She did not know the name of the vaccine nor the name of the manufacturer. She had understood that the vaccination project had been nationwide in Kwandia and had been largely funded by an American foundation sponsored by one of those 'billionaire types' as she put it. She believed it was called The Doorstep Foundation. A strange name she had thought but had no idea who was behind it. What she did know, however, was that her husband Simon had been mightily put out by the operation because local aid funds had been diverted from his own Charity's projects to the vaccination programme. He had been overseeing a number of projects around the country in partnership with a large Water Aid organisation drilling bore holes to bring fresh water to dozens of villages. In his opinion, the health benefits of these projects would far outweigh those of mass vaccination but did not catch the imagination or get noticed by the international press in quite the same way.

He left her with a number of questions, which she said she would pass on to her husband in their next email exchange and she would get back to him. In the meantime, Ford decided to find out what he could about The Doorstep Foundation. Mister Google led him to their website, from which he learned it was a charitable foundation set up by Jim Doors, one of the richest men in the world. As with many such sites, it was long on self-promotion but short on facts, and there was no mention of Kwandia or the current project.

There were several pictures of the great benefactor himself and his wife, Maddie, kitted out in tropical gear and surrounded by African children, with Maddie herself holding a baby in her arms. It did not name the country where the photo was taken, and it looked like a typical public relations shot. To the eyes of the African, Dr Ford, there was something odd about these pictures, and he even began to wonder whether they were actually taken in Africa at all. It would not be too difficult to mock up such a scene in parts of Texas. He scolded himself for being so cynical. After all, he had no objection in principle to this man spending some of his billions helping the poor of the world.

He did not expect a reply from Kate Fellowes for a couple of days but decided that in the meantime, he would try another avenue of inquiry. It was about time he looked up his old friend from University who had also been best man at his wedding. Declan Walsh was now an independent journalist but mostly working with a major news agency specialising in scientific and medical matters. He was from Limerick in Ireland and had formed a strong friendship with Ford when they were at Cambridge. So much so that the African's elocution course, which he had pursued with a single-minded determination to acquire a faultless English accent, had failed to prevent him from using the occasional Irish turn of phrase without him realising it.

They met for lunch at the upstairs room of a gastropub not far from Harley Street. The food was good, and the tables were sufficiently spaced out for private conversations. They exchanged the usual pleasantries about their respective well-being, and Dec, as he was known, asked fondly after the 'delectable Alice' whilst waiving aside Ford's questions about his own latest relationship and whether he had any plans to 'settle down' at last.

They had dispatched the first course before Dec

referred to the telephone call which had set up the lunch. "So, what's your interest in Jim Doors, Robbie?" Dec would usually call his friend Rob, but when he used the name Robbie, there was a whimsical note to his voice, suggesting a slight lack of seriousness. His friend's tone soon corrected that, however.

He quickly explained to Dec about young Julian Fellowes and such information as he had been able to glean from his mother about the vaccine project in Kwandia. "Apparently, it is bankrolled by an American foundation set up by this Jim Doors."

Dec listened carefully. "You seem to have found out quite a lot already. I don't know that I can add a whole lot more."

Rob was a bit disappointed with this reply but tried another tack. "From what you know, why should this man have chosen this project to support and why this particular country?" Declan did not really know the answers to either of these questions but briefly summarised what he had discovered about Doors following Rob's telephone call.

"Firstly, he did not start out life with nothing although, of course, his inherited wealth was nowhere near the billions he has today. His father owned one of the biggest ranches in Texas and was a wealthy man in his own right. He was also a prominent member of the American Eugenics Society, and it is highly likely that his son may have inherited similar beliefs. Don't forget that many of the medical programmes carried out in the third world have an underlying aim of population control although from what you tell me there is no obvious connection with this project."

Rob was not quite so sure. Dec's mention of Eugenics was interesting. At university, he had learnt that Eugenics was a largely discredited set of beliefs and practices based on the theory that certain characteristics in humans were more desirable than others and that our species could be improved by selective breeding. Unfortunately, such beliefs had led not only to overt racism but also to mass extinctions of whole populations. It had also given rise to programmes of forced sterilisation back in the 1920s and 1930s. Rob also knew that more recently, some vaccination projects in the third world had been used as a form of covert contraception. Presumably, this is what Dec was referring to with his last comment about 'population control'.

He raised his doubts with Dec, who pondered the question further but then shook his head. "Anything is possible, of course, but what is there to gain from it? Doors is a man who rarely does anything without a commercial payback for himself. At the moment, I can't see where that is coming from."

"There is another thing. In recent years, Doors has been buying up farmland in America and elsewhere in the world. Apparently, he is one of the biggest farmland owners in America. It is not clear why a man whose fortune was made in shoes and then prestige office blocks in major cities should be doing this."

Interesting though it was, neither man could see the relevance of this information to the vaccine project or even to Kwandia since more than half of the country was comprised of desert.

Dec was sorry he could not be more help and enquired what his friend was going to do next.

"My primary interest is to get my patient better. I should like to find out what vaccine he had and what it contained. I have asked his mother to find out its name and who makes it."

Dec understood, but his journalist's nose was twitching. "Let me know when you find out, and I will do some more digging. It will be interesting to find out whether Doors or his foundation have any financial interest in this vaccine. 'Follow the money' is a well-worn saying, but more often than not, it comes up with the right answer."

# Chapter 3 - The Vaccine

It wasn't until the following morning that he received an email from Kate Fellowes, which in fact was just a forwarded message from her husband Simon. He had discovered that the vaccine was called Bercuvax and distributed by a company called Kwanpharm registered in Dubai.

His Google search for Bercuvax yielded a blank, and the vaccine was not listed in the latest edition of the International Pharmacopoeia to which he subscribed. The search for Kwanpharm proved slightly more informative, but only slightly. The company had a website, but it mostly consisted of boilerplate phrases setting out their mission and their vision and explaining that they were 'in the business of improving care'. However, it said very little about the company or its products, and there were no physical or online addresses. There was only an online form which could be used to contact them, designed, it would appear, mostly for those who might be interested in becoming 'partners', which was presumably a fancy word for sub-distributors.

Rob decided to use the form to send them an inquiry.

*I understand your company distributes a vaccine called Bercuvax, which is currently being administered to the population of*

*Kwandia under the auspices of an NGO called The Doorstep Foundation. I am a doctor practising in Harley Street, London, England and was recently consulted by a patient presenting with disease symptoms directly after being vaccinated in Kwandia. For me to assess the appropriate treatment for my patient, I would be grateful if you would provide me with a full list of the ingredients in your vaccine. I should also be interested to learn whether clinical trials caused any side effects in patients and how many instances of disease have occurred during the current innoculation program. In view of the urgency, I shall be grateful for a prompt reply.*

He included his name, postal and email addresses and surgery telephone number.

The following day, he received an emailed reply. Pretty prompt by African standards but, unfortunately, not very helpful.

*Thank you for your enquiry. Please understand that our company acts purely as a distributor of the product to which you refer and, as such, cannot deal with technical enquiries. We respectfully suggest that you contact the manufacturers regarding details of this nature. They are ME Chemicals LLC, Dubai Healthcare City, PO BOX 4700281, Dubai, UAE.*

Rob immediately Googled ME Chemicals LLC and discovered that whilst the company seemed to operate from Dubai, it was actually registered in Delaware, USA. There was an email address, so he promptly sent off an almost identical email to that which he had sent to Kwanpharm, asking much the same questions.

Again, the reply came a day later by email. Again, it was polite and respectful but failed to give him the key information he sought.

> *Thank you for your email. Our company manufactures Bercuvax under licence, the contractual terms of which prevent us from disclosing its formula or list of ingredients. We can assure you, however, that it contains no substances which could produce the symptoms you describe. Furthermore, the vaccine has been specifically approved by the medical authorities of Kwandia after extensive clinical trials, which caused no serious side effects in trial subjects. The programme is supported by MAGIC (The Medical Alliance for Global Infection Control), which has supplied some funding and advisory staff to the health service in Kwandia.*
> *We wish your patient a speedy recovery.*

The email was signed in the company's name and appeared to close off all avenues to any further communication. It was time to call on Dec's assistance once again. Instead of phoning him, he decided to forward the email correspondence he had had with the two companies, adding his own short message.

*Any information you can find out about the*
*following would be helpful:-*
*Bercuvax*
*Kwanpharm*
*ME Chemicals LLC*
*MAGIC*

*Best of luck*
*Rob*

This time, he did not expect a prompt reply as he assumed Dec would need to make a number of enquiries to follow this up. A week later, Dec called and invited himself to the surgery in Harley Street.

Mary had always had a soft spot for Dec and gave him one of her rare beaming smiles, which Rob knew were reserved for special occasions or special people. Was it the mutual bonding of two Celts, or was it simply Dec's undeniable Irish charm and good looks? Rob believed it was the latter. She quickly reverted to her business manner, and the formality of her announcement led Rob to believe that his next patient was either Royalty or the Prime Minister, at the very least.
"Mr Walsh to see you, Doctor"

Dec raised his eyebrows at this introduction before entering the room and shaking hands warmly with his friend. "Nice to see that Mary seems to have everything under control." Rob smiled. Dec continued, "By everything, I mean you, my friend. She seems to be as efficient as ever."

Rob laughed "That she is," sounding more like his Irish friend than he realised. How was it that Dec was so infectious?

But there was no time to waste. "What have you got for me?"

Dec had brought with him a smart document case and withdrew a folder containing a sheaf of papers.

"First up, Bercuvax. No one has ever heard of it. I tried medical contacts and scientific correspondents. I looked up all the pharmacopoeias I could think of and all the major Patent registers. Nothing. It must be an experimental product, and it's flying under the radar for some reason.  The question is, why?"

Rob nodded. "Why indeed?" He did not like what he was hearing, but Dec was on to his next subject.

"Kwanpharm. All I can tell you is that the company has been licensed for two years as an overseas distributor. Unfortunately, in the UAE, there is no information on shareholders, directors or any other useful corporate details such as share capital or financial results. So, not much further forward."

Rob shrugged his shoulders. "Why am I not

surprised?" His tone was light, but his mood was becoming a little depressed. "What about ME Chemicals?"

Dec delved into his folder and withdrew an A4 sheet of paper. His friend looked more hopeful but was about to be disappointed. "Not much better, I'm afraid. Delaware corporations are even better than the Cayman Islands for concealing company ownership and management. If they trade outside Delaware, they don't even have to register for local state taxes."

Rob sighed, but Dec held up his hand with a finger in the air. "But wait for it! We have found out a bit more about the company, and we have a name. It does have a small manufacturing facility in Dubai, although its main products appear to be copies of common generic medicines whose patents have long since expired. There is no history of vaccine manufacture. However, this is the most interesting bit. The head honcho on site appears to be one Professor Rafal Glik."

This information was received without much enthusiasm by Rob, but his friend continued. "I did some digging on Professor Glik. He has worked all over the world for many of the big pharma companies, but as a young man, probably in his late twenties, he was implicated in some of the infamous illegal testing performed in South Africa and Zimbabwe. There were a number of clinical trials carried out lacking informed consent as well as forced medical procedures. Legal proceedings dragged on for years, and large sums of compensation were paid. It was not the pharmaceutical industry's finest hour."

"Do you think that's what is going on here?"

"We mustn't jump to conclusions, but there is more. I looked up the Kwandian Medicine Regulatory Authority, and who do you think is listed as an adviser?"

Dec did not wait for an answer. "Right first time. Professor Rafal Glik, none other."

"You also asked me for more information on MAGIC."

Rob knew of MAGIC and had heard of its work supporting health initiatives in third-world countries, including vaccination programmes. However, like most people, he did not know much about its constitution or how it worked and what role it might play in the Kwandia programme.

More papers were withdrawn from Dec's folder. This time, he handed them over to Rob. "To be studied at your leisure, but I will give you a brief run down and, wait for it again, one more very interesting fact."

Rob suppressed a sigh and smiled instead. He was becoming used to his friend's dramatics.

"MAGIC, or to give it its full title, The Medical

Alliance for Global Infection Control, is described as a public-private health partnership, whatever that is. Its stated goal is to improve access to medicines and vaccines in the poorer countries of the world. Actually, on your behalf, I spent several hours trying to understand how it all works. The word 'complicated' doesn't do it justice. Basically, it seems that MAGIC will facilitate partnerships between governments and private entities, including NGOs, to provide medicines and vaccine programmes. Rob interrupted, "By NGOs, you mean organisations like The Doorstep Foundation."

"Exactly right."

"But what do they get out of it?"

"Prestige, influence, publicity. Who knows? But there is always a commercial enterprise in the equation, and they will be looking for a financial return."

Rob was beginning to see the picture. "Such as ME Chemicals, perhaps."

Dec grinned. "Well, quite possibly. I have more on MAGIC." Rob was now all ears.

"The board of MAGIC is made up of the great and the good. Politicians, internationally acclaimed academics in medicine and science, international bankers, etc, but they only meet a few times a year in Switzerland, New York or any prestigious location which can put them up in the five-star luxury hotels, which are, of course, essential facilities needed for discussing the world's poor and sick."

Rob smiled at his friend's cynicism, but he took the point.

"Like many such organisations, the board labours under the illusion it is exercising the ultimate power, but in reality, it only discusses and votes on whatever is fed to them by their full-time underlings who act as the secretariat for the board and for all the sub-committees who report upwards. The most important of these is the Programme and Policy Committee, who basically initiate all of the projects put before the board. And guess what?!" Dec paused for effect. "The chair of this committee is none other than Professor Rafal Glik."

It was clear to Rob that his friend's journalistic instincts were now on full alert as he smelt the possibility of a good story and potential exposé. He, too, felt a distinct sense of unease about the situation in Kwandia but was still unsure how the facts that Dec had unearthed would help him to treat his young patient. He was no further forward in discovering the ingredients of the mysterious vaccine, which, for him, was key to progress.

"Where do we go from here, Dec? Should I write to this Professor Glik?"

Dec shrugged his shoulders. "Waste of time, I should

think. He must already be aware of your letter to ME Chemicals. You will only get a similar buck-passing reply." He leaned forward with a more earnest expression on his face. "Besides, I think you should take a step back. Keep a low profile. Let me do some more ferreting. I have other lines of enquiry to pursue yet."

Rob sat back with a resigned smile. "So, you don't want me involved?" It was a statement rather than a question, but Dec quickly jumped in.

"I don't want you exposed."

"What do you mean 'exposed'?"

"Exposed to danger, my friend. This is not just about a small English kid getting an infection. I smell something much bigger here. There may be serious money involved, not to mention political ramifications. Believe me, these people may not be nice to know. They don't play by the rules if you understand me."

"Then maybe you shouldn't be 'exposed' either. We should just report our findings to a higher authority and walk away." Even as he spoke, Rob knew that he was wasting his breath.

"I am not ready to do that yet, but then I don't have much to lose. You have a lovely wife and two beautiful daughters. You must definitely stay under the radar."

The Cadaver and The Shark

# Chapter - Break-in

He had seen his last patient for the day, and he and Mary left the surgery premises together after Mary had locked up. They walked down the passageway to the outside door of the building. She wished him good night and headed towards Bond Street underground station. Rob went in the opposite direction, taking a leisurely stroll towards home, a listed terraced house near Regents Park whose price range would normally be out of reach even for a top Harley Street consultant. A significant trust fund from one of Alice's many rich aunts had matured just at the right time for them to purchase the property and set up the Harley Street practice. How lucky he was that his beloved Alice seemed to generate a special degree of affection from every member of her family, including a clutch of wealthy aunts and uncles.

The walk home was normally enjoyable. It was a chance to unwind and mull over events, both work-related and domestic. Sometimes, he would even extend the walk by taking a pleasant detour through the park. He did so this evening but could not enjoy the birdsong or watch the children playing. The earlier conversation with Dec was now monopolising his every thought. It was no use pretending that Dec's final warning had not unsettled him. He knew his friend well enough to know that he would pursue this story relentlessly like a huntsman after the fox, and he also knew that he would justify his interest by claiming the chance of a journalistic coup that could transform his career. However, there was also a moral crusader side to Dec, which would also be a motivating factor.

He wondered about his own feelings. He certainly shared Dec's misgivings about the possible exploitation of innocent Africans by major pharmaceutical interests. He had heard of such allegations in the past, but now, a potential case of epic proportions appeared to have landed on his doorstep. Should he tell Alice? But if so, what exactly should he tell her? As a rule, he never discussed his work with Alice other than in the most general terms. After all, patient confidentiality meant just that, even from one's wife. But this was different. The implications of what they thought might be happening went well beyond his patient. But what was happening? The harsh truth was that he had no actual facts, only conjecture. He convinced himself that there was absolutely no point in worrying Alice unduly. He decided to say nothing.

That decision might have been different if he had noticed two men who had followed him from the surgery and who had surreptitiously taken photos of his front door on their mobile phones immediately after he had closed it behind him.

**********************************

On the following morning, he had barely sat down in his chair when Mary came in to see him and sat down in the chair usually reserved for patients. "May I ask you something, Rob?"

It was an unusual request from Mary, and the look of concern on her face immediately made him uneasy. She had never troubled him with any personal matters, and he hoped she was not about to start now. His medical training had included some patient care and old-fashioned bedside manner, but nothing had ever prepared him for managing staff or dealing with their problems. Nevertheless, he nodded in what he hoped was a sympathetic manner.

To his surprise, her first question was followed up by another. "Did you come back to the surgery last night after we had left?"

He looked at her blankly. "No, what makes you think that?"

"Well, I am pretty certain that somebody has been in here, and it wasn't the cleaner because she left 10 minutes before us last night."

"Is anything missing?"

"Not that I can see, but my desk is not as I left it. I am certain of that. Papers have been moved, and the telephone has been moved to a side table. The appointments diary is certainly not where I left it."

Rob just stopped himself from asking if she was absolutely sure. Of course, she was. This was Mary, and her powers of observation were unsurpassed. She stood up and looked around her. "What about this room? Has anything been moved or taken?" Rob hesitated. He did not notice things the way Mary did. His mind was usually reviewing the symptoms of his last patient or contemplating the next. At least, that is what he told himself. He knew, however, that even when off duty at home or visiting friends, his wife would notice things which he did not. It was a fact she had often pointed out.

His first thought was the medicine cabinet. He produced the key from his pocket and unlocked it. The small stock of emergency drugs appeared to be untouched. The lower half of the cupboard consisted of a refrigerator for those medicines which needed to be stored below room temperature. There was no separate lock, but again, nothing appeared to have been disturbed or missing, although he would ask Mary to do a quick inventory just to be sure. Looking around the room, he could see nothing out of place, though he wasn't absolutely sure. His stethoscope was on his desktop, whereas he usually put it away in the top left drawer. However, he sometimes forgot.

"Nothing stands out."

But Mary was unconvinced. She knew her boss. "I think we should call the police." She was now in earnest.

"Not yet. Let us think it through. What are we going

to tell them? After all, nothing appears to be stolen." Something told him that police involvement would not be the right move. "We should find out whether any of the other occupants have had a break-in." Rob's surgery was on the ground floor and consisted of just two rooms: Mary's office, which also served as a waiting room and his consulting room, accessed from the office. The building had three floors and was shared with four other consultants, each offering a different branch of medical specialism. Mary was dispatched to talk to them.

In the meantime, he phoned Dec. But Dec was out, so he left a message. He was unsurprised when Mary returned with the news that no other occupant had been broken into. One of the other consultants had told her "they were probably after drugs", but even to Mary, this did not ring true. There had been no sign of a forced entry and very little disturbance. It was too professional for a bunch of drug addicts.

The very same thought had occurred to Rob, and it was a thought which disturbed him greatly. He managed to turn his mind to that morning's patients and, for the moment, put Mary off calling the police. At lunchtime, he bought himself a sandwich and walked down to Cavendish Square Gardens at the end of Harley Street. Sitting on a park bench, he took out his mobile and tried again to ring Dec. This time, he was lucky.

He told him about the suspected break-in at the surgery, and Dec listened without comment until he had finished. "Where are you phoning from?" Rob was surprised by the question but explained that he was on a park bench in a garden square. "Good. Meet me for lunch tomorrow. 12.30, usual pub. Don't contact the police." He then rang off, leaving Rob in an even greater state of disquiet than before. If he had hoped for reassurance from his friend, the abrupt nature of that telephone call did not provide it. He returned to his surgery a very worried man.

That evening, he approached his front door with a degree of apprehension, but it was soon dispelled by the normal welcome from Alice and the girls, the latter both anxious to tell him of their respective successes at school that day. There was nothing untoward, and nothing seemed out of place. He eventually went to bed with a sense of relief and fell asleep, wondering what Dec would have to tell him tomorrow.

*******************************************

When he arrived at the restaurant, Dec was already seated at a table discreetly positioned in an alcove where they could talk in a reasonable degree of privacy. A bottle of red wine was open in front of him. He poured a glass for Rob, who sat down and began to relax. However, almost before he had said 'Hello,' Dec fired a question at him, "Were you followed?" Rob was taken aback but shook his head. "I don't think so, but then I wasn't really looking." Dec smiled. "No, I don't suppose you were. But from now on, you had better start looking."

Rob returned to his worried state. "Dec, what is going on? What are you saying?" Dec was showing signs of impatience with his friend. "You don't read many spy thrillers, do you?" Rob shook his head. "Well, if you did, you would know that if a break-in occurs and nothing is stolen, then it means that something may have been left behind." Before Rob could reply, Dec went on, "And if someone is going to that sort of trouble, then it is also likely that they are keeping tabs on your movements. They want to know what you are up to."

Rob could not quite believe what he was hearing. He had lost all appetite for food but took a mouthful of the lasagne he had ordered simply to buy himself some time to think. Dec delved into the document case that he had brought with him and withdrew a mobile phone. He slid it across the table to his friend. "From now on, you use this phone to contact me and only this phone. There's fifty quid loaded up and a secure messenger app installed. When you have nearly used all the data, let me know, and I will replace the SIM card. Never use it in your surgery or your home. Always phone from a discreet location if possible. That park is OK."

Dec was in full flow. "Tomorrow, you will get a visit from Mr Lawrence Mackenzie. He is doing me a favour, so be nice to him. These exercises normally cost around five grand a time minimum. He will sweep your surgery and office for any bugs and listening devices. I have asked him to report what he finds but not to dismantle or destroy any device he discovers. If we switch anything off, it will only raise your profile with our friends as a potential troublemaker, and at this stage, I should prefer them to think of you as a perfectly innocent doctor." He couldn't help himself from adding with a smile, "Which is, of course, exactly what you are."

"At lunchtime, I want you to let him into your house, and he will repeat the exercise. Do not travel with him; go separately."

"You think the house is bugged as well? There has been no sign of a break-in?" This was getting all too close to home for Rob's liking. He began to wonder what he had got himself into. All he had done was make a perfectly normal enquiry as a medical professional to a pharmaceutical company, and now he appeared to be caught up in international espionage. What's more, he was no further forward in discovering what he really wanted to know, that is to say, the ingredients of this mysterious vaccine.

# Chapter 5 - Mr Mackenzie

The following morning Rob intercepted Mary before she could enter the building. Mary's furrowed brow was a hybrid. A cross between disapproval on the one hand and concern on the other as she listened to Rob's explanation that the reason for the break-in at the surgery was to plant listening devices. "So, when is this gentleman coming in?" Her tone still contained a measure of disbelief.

"This morning after I have seen my patient", Rob tried to sound as matter of fact as he could, but underneath, he was worried. It was not so much the thought of his surgery being bugged but the suggestion that they had been into his home. Although Mackenzie would go to his house when Alice was at work and the girls were at school, what would he do if they found something? He would have to tell Alice what was happening or at least some of it.

He thought back to his conversation at lunch yesterday and reflected on the fact that Dec had offered no suggestion as to who exactly was carrying out the bugging of his premises and what they were hoping to learn.

Mackenzie arrived at the appointed hour, a short, bespectacled man of around forty accompanied by a taller, younger man. Both carried what appeared to be regular attaché cases, but Rob assumed to contain all manner of electronic equipment. He had been coached by Dec on what to say, and Mary had been briefed to stay silent. Mackenzie opened the conversation, "We're here to install the electrocardiograph, Dr Renshaw." Rob smiled. "Then I am afraid you are in the wrong place, my friend. Dr Renshaw is upstairs on the first floor." Mackenzie's companion entered the corridor, closing the door with a thud. After checking that the surgery was not being watched, he returned as silently as possible and closed the door carefully. When they began to work, Rob decided to make himself scarce and motioned to Mary to accompany him.

He looked around in the street for possible observers, but there were no obvious candidates, at least to the untrained eye. In the coffee shop round the corner, they sat at a low table out of earshot of the other customers. "What really is going on, Rob? Why do you think we are being bugged?"

Rob thought for a moment, unsure exactly how to answer the question. It was partly because he did not know the answer himself and because what he did know or thought he knew was largely speculation. Nevertheless, he needed Mary's cooperation, and she had a right to know something. He chose his words carefully. "My enquiries about the vaccine given to the boy Julian Fellowes appear to have ruffled some feathers. We don't exactly know why, but it is possible there is a clinical trial being carried out in Africa with an unapproved experimental vaccine. If that came to light, it would be extremely damaging for the pharmaceutical companies involved and embarrassing for the local medical authorities. There could be a lot at stake for some high-profile players. My innocent questions could have scared them into thinking I might expose what is happening. Therefore, they want to find out how much I know and monitor any further investigation I might carry out."

"And will you?"

"Will I what?"

"Carry out further investigation?" Mary sensed the danger here. "After all, you know what the boy is suffering from, and he is responding to treatment, so what is there to gain from further investigation? I don't like the sound of these people, and why put yourself in any danger? You could simply walk away."

For a moment, Rob pondered on Mary's remarks. "I am not sure I can now. First, I cannot be certain about Julian's state of health without knowing what might be in that vaccine. Secondly, can I really stand by and allow a whole nation to be subjected to an uncontrolled medical experiment which could cause untold illness and possibly thousands of deaths?"

Before he could continue, Mary interrupted. "And thirdly, young Mr Walsh smells a possible major scoop

and is very unlikely to pass up a chance like this."
Rob laughed. "In fairness, he wants me kept out of it or 'under the radar' as he puts it, but I am afraid my questions have put me in the spotlight."

**********************************

The following morning, there was a WhatsApp message from Dec on the burner phone with instructions to lunch at their normal place. Rob had hardly sat down before Dec drew out a couple of A4 sheets from his folio case.

"Mackenzie's report, I assume?"

Dec nodded but did not pass it over. He read out a list of four devices found in the surgery and no less than eight planted all over his house.

Rob was astonished. "Why so many at home?"

"They are very thorough, my friend. Your house has more rooms, and they don't want any blank spots if they can help it. We are certainly dealing with professionals here."

"So, what do we do?"

"Nothing. Mackenzie agrees with me. If we disable them, they will know we are on to them, and that could be more dangerous than simply carrying on as if nothing has happened."

Rob saw the point, but at the same time, he did not like the idea that someone was listening to his every conversation, both at work and at home. "I shall have to tell Alice now."

Dec agreed but had another question. "When do the girls break up from school?"

"Next week, as it happens, why?"

"Any chance of you all taking a little holiday down in Sussex? You always tell me how fond Alice's parents are of their granddaughters. I'm sure they would like to see them for a few days."

Rob thought over the idea, but Dec continued before he could reply. "Does your father-in-law still have any connections in the foreign office?"

"I can ask. Why do you want to know?"

"Some inside information on Kwandia might be helpful. I am not sure this is all about vaccines. There may well be a political angle, but I haven't the faintest idea what it could be. We need to know who pulls the strings down there and if there is any unrest in the country. Most African states have something going on, as you will know better than most. On the face of it, Kwandia has been relatively stable for some time, but you can never be sure."

\*\*\*\*\*\*\*\*\*\*\*\*\*\*\*\*\*\*\*\*\*\*\*\*\*\*\*\*\*\*\*\*\*\*\*\*

Alice and the girls expressed delight and surprise as the prospect of a holiday in Sussex was put to them over the dinner table that evening. Alice was due some leave from the city investment house for which she worked managing funds for what were termed 'high net worth' clients. It was only after the girls had gone to bed and she had been invited out for a drink in their small garden that the smiles turned to frowns, and her face clouded over. Those clouds got darker, and the frowns got deeper as her husband explained about the young patient from Kwandia and the suspicious vaccine being administered in that country. But what really sent a chill down her spine was the news that her house was bugged and that this was the underlying reason for a holiday with her parents. She felt as if she wanted to leave there and then.

She was under strict orders not to mention a word of what she had been told, even to her parents.

The following day, Rob arranged to visit Julian Fellowes in the hospital to check on his progress. He had an ulterior motive, which was to ask a potential favour of his mother.

"I will ask Simon what he can do" was Kate Fellowes's response to his request. "He has good contacts with a number of senior medical officers there, and it should not be too difficult to get hold of some samples of the vaccine. Getting them here might not be so easy, though. Don't these things have to be transported at specific temperatures?"

Rob shrugged his shoulders. "Not necessarily. It depends on the vaccine, and I don't know much about this one. In any case, I am not planning to use it. I only want it for laboratory analysis to determine precisely what is in it."

Kate was eager to be of help. "I will email Simon tonight. By the way, he is coming home next week for ten days of compassionate leave. If you can wait until then, he can bring it with him. Probably the safest way."

Ideally, Rob would have liked it sooner, but on balance, this seemed like the best bet.

# Chapter 6 - Rodmell

Rodmell is a small village nestling in the South Downs in the lower valley of the River Ouse. It is always described as a village of character. Rob had come to learn that this was estate agent speak for 'upmarket' with property prices to match. Over the years, it has been home to many figures from the worlds of academia, arts and literature. Its most famous resident had been Virginia Woolf, the writer, and it was from Monk's House in the centre of the village that on 28th March 1941, Virginia filled her coat pockets with stones and walked down to the River Ouse to drown herself. Following the death of her husband, Leonard, the property was taken over by The National Trust and opened to the public for two days a week as a small museum dedicated to the writer. However, Rob was not aiming for Monk's House but another residence further down the lane.

As he drove across the Downs, Rob's mind was unconcerned with an event which took place seventy-five years ago but very much focused on the present and the immediate future. He had spent the night with the family at his in-law's farm no more than thirty minutes' drive from Rodmell. He felt pleased that he had set a couple of balls rolling. Firstly, and most importantly, he now had a realistic hope of getting his hands on a vaccine sample, thanks to Simon Fellowes. Secondly, his father-in-law had jumped at the chance of contacting a former colleague to find out the current situation in Kwandia. The conversation had been easier than he had imagined, and he had not disclosed the real purpose behind his enquiry. Fortunately, Sir Richard Prentice had not pressed him on the matter.

He turned his car into the spacious driveway of Cedar Lodge and crunched across the gravel until he was beside a red Mazda sports car, which he recognised as belonging to his good friend Declan. The front door was opened by a shortish, sturdy woman with steel-grey hair, twinkling blue eyes, and an olive-tinged complexion. In appearance, she could have been French, but when she spoke, her cut-glass accent was unmistakably English. Rob thought she sounded like the Queen.

"Dr Ford, I presume. Please come in. Your friend has only just arrived."

He was led along a short hallway into a pleasant lounge furnished with comfortable armchairs and wall-to-wall bookcases. He suspected that bookcases lined the walls of many, if not every, room in the house. Dec jumped to his feet when his friend appeared, but Professor Owen Lewis took longer to rise to his feet. Rob guessed he was a little older than his wife, probably in his mid-seventies, but his face was alert and his handshake firm. He was only five feet eight inches tall, though, and Rob towered above him. Rob noticed two full cups on the coffee table, and the professor's wife brought one for Rob and offered him milk and sugar, both of which he refused. As she left the room, she made what Rob thought was a rather odd comment. "I will just go and check Owen, and then leave you to it."

After a few pleasantries concerning their respective drives across the Sussex Downs, they got down to business. Dec had found the professor through a journalist colleague who told him, "If anyone can identify a rogue vaccine, he would be your best bet. He is also no friend of big pharma, having been kicked out of a top job through blowing the whistle on some dodgy clinical trials in Africa." Declan contacted him, and he took the lead as he had arranged the meeting. "It was very good of you to see us, Professor Lewis. We greatly appreciate it." The professor nodded in acknowledgement and smiled. He seemed particularly intrigued by Rob. "Are you from Kwandia, Doctor Ford?"

Rob smiled back at the professor. "No, I am originally from Zambia but have lived in England for over twenty years." For good measure, he added, "I have a private practice in Harley Street."

The professor looked suitably impressed. He appeared to be gathering his thoughts to start the conversation when his wife slipped back into the room. She leant forward and whispered in his ear. Rob thought he heard the words "All Clear". Seeing the puzzled look on his face, the professor decided to explain. "I am afraid we have become paranoid in recent years. My wife was concerned you may have been followed down here or observed visiting us. She has just been out to see if there were any strange cars parked up the road. Thankfully, she has nothing suspicious to report."

Regrettably, she had either not noticed a young couple strolling through the village or simply assumed they were tourists looking perhaps for Monk's House. Even though the latter was only open to visitors for two days in the week, it did not stop people from coming at other times simply to stare at the cottage from the roadway and generally enjoy the ambience of this sleepy but well-kept corner of Sussex. She was not to know that this innocent-looking couple were not what they seemed.

The professor turned his attention back to Rob. He spoke with the authority of one accustomed to giving orders but also with the precision of a senior academic scientist. "In arranging this meeting, your colleague explained the circumstances of the young patient you have been treating and, in particular, the efforts you have made to establish the contents of the vaccine with which he has been innoculated. Before we discuss the matter, I think I should provide some details of my background and the potential risks you might be running in being known to contact me."

Rob nodded. "I feel we are already at risk." He glanced across at Dec for reassurance. "My surgery and my house have both been bugged."

Professor Lewis raised his eyebrows. "Then you

will begin to understand the type of people we are dealing with here." He leant back into his chair. "For more than ten years, I was Head of Research at Hague Chemicals, which at the time was the fourth largest pharmaceutical company in the world until it was bought out by the Americans. The attraction for the buyer was the patent rights we held to no fewer than six drugs, which were leaders in their field. The big sellers were two cardiovascular drugs and two cancer drugs. The other two were certainly brand leaders in the medical sense, but for rarer diseases, they were not so commercially profitable. You will also appreciate that the commercial success of a pharmaceutical company is highly dependent on its ability to discover and develop new medicines. Everyone is searching for the holy grail, or that is to say, the next blockbuster drug."

Dec and Rob both nodded but said nothing, and the professor continued.

"Research in such companies is a highly pressurised and sensitive environment, and the Head of Research carries much of that pressure on his shoulders. Unfortunately, extreme pressure can sometimes generate unscrupulous measures. I began to realise that industrial espionage, data manipulation and unethical risk-taking levels were not uncommon in the pharmaceutical world.

In 2012, we were experimenting with a new antibiotic drug against meningitis. It was still in the early stages of development, but the team responsible for the project grew impatient. They wanted results. Unbeknownst to me, they did a deal with a West African state offering the drug at a virtual give-away price. In exchange, the Africans would waive medical regulations to enable the company to conduct clinical trials on a section of their population."

The Professor paused and fixed his eyes on Rob. "I am ashamed to say that I later discovered a whole history of experimental trials being carried out on the people of your continent going back a hundred years or more. Unsurprisingly, African people are always the most reluctant to step forward when new medicines or vaccines are offered."

Rob said nothing, but his mind flashed back to Doctor Fiesta and the polio vaccine, which he thought may have saved his life.

The Professor continued. "Of course, the clinical trials were a disaster. A number of children died, and dozens more suffered life-changing disabilities such as blindness and brain damage. I was horrified when I found out and threatened the project leader with dismissal. However, the individual concerned took his case to a higher authority in the company, which was effectively the Board level. To my amazement, they sided with him and largely ignored my protests. At this point, I realised that profit outranked medical ethics in my company, and it put me in a difficult position. But things were to get worse."

"Who was the project leader?" It was Dec who asked the question, but Rob felt that his friend already knew the answer.

"Professor Rafal Glik."

Rob now understood why Dec had wanted him to meet Professor Lewis. "You said that things got worse?"

The Professor composed himself. It was clear that he found just talking about the events of four years ago caused him distress. "As a result of my protests, I found myself effectively moved sideways in the company. I retained my job title, but that was about all. Meetings took place without my knowledge. Glik seemed to do as he liked, frequently going over my head and instigating projects without my consent. My position was becoming untenable, and short of resigning, I did not know what to do."

Declan and Rob offered sympathy. "What else could you do?"

"Well, I felt that resigning would be like giving in. Besides, I also believed there was much more at stake here than just my own position. This had the makings of a major public scandal and an international one at that. The only course of action I could think of was contacting people outside the company for advice and, hopefully, support. Many of these were fellow professionals in academia or working for medical journals and even global health organisations like MAGIC, for example. Some I had known for years and included former colleagues. I realised that such action carried risks for my own position within the company and, regrettably, so it proved. Whilst many of my contacts were sympathetic to my predicament, their main advice was to keep my head down and soldier on."

Declan could immediately see where this was going. "Let me guess. Word got back to your company?"

The Professor nodded. "Exactly right. I was called up before one of the directors and openly accused of leaking confidential information. Denying it was useless. The mere accusation would compromise my position in the company, and my reputation in the industry would be destroyed. To cut a long story short, I was forced to accept a redundancy package and bring forward my 'retirement'. I admit the package was not ungenerous, and at least I would be financially secure. The director was pleased with the outcome and thought that would be the end of it. In fact, so did I"

Declan was there before him. "But it was only the start of it."

"You are right again, Mr Walsh. I was contacted out of the blue by a reporter from one of the international news agencies asking about a medical trial which had gone wrong in America using children in an orphanage. In fact, I had no knowledge of the case, and so far as I knew, my old company was not involved, but I was asked to comment on the ethics of carrying out such trials. The journalist's article was picked up by several national newspapers both here and in the US, and my comments were prominently reported. My old colleagues picked up on the article, and it must have dawned on them that I could be a danger to the company. In fact, I was maybe more dangerous outside the company than within it, where they could keep an eye on me and have some control over me."

It was Rob who interrupted this time. "But surely you were made to sign some sort of 'non-disclosure' agreement as part of your leaving package?"

"Of course, I signed an agreement to cover confidentiality relating to our pipeline of products, which also included non-competition clauses, etc, but we are talking here about illegal acts. You can hardly include those in a legal agreement. Furthermore, having left the company, it would be difficult to pin down any information leak directly to me."

Declan jumped in again. "But you knew where the bodies were buried! Literally!"

The professor gave a rather wan smile. "That's one way of putting it."

He continued. "What really worried them was when they realised I had been contacted by other medical professionals who had received similar treatment to myself and journalists with a medical background who were making a career out of investigating the darker side of the pharmaceutical industry. There is a whole network out there which I never knew existed."

He sighed. "Unfortunately, this brought with it a whole load of trouble. We were certain our house was being watched, and we were equally sure it was broken into while we were away. And then there was Buster."

"Buster?"

"Yes, our lovely golden retriever. We came back one day to find him shot dead right down at the bottom of our garden where it borders the fields."

"Did you report it to the police?"

"We certainly did, and I am afraid that simply added to our unease. At first, the local 'bobbie' took quite an interest and promised a full investigation. But then it seemed to drag, and eventually, they came back with some story that the dog had been worrying sheep, which is why he had been shot. It was nonsense. Buster had never escaped from our garden before, nor had he ever shown much interest in sheep when out for walks. I spoke to the farmer who owns the adjoining field, whom I happen to know quite well. He denied all knowledge of shooting my dog and also assured me that the police had not interviewed him."

Rob was becoming increasingly discomfited by the Professor's story. "Presumably, you believe this was done as a warning?"

"Most certainly and for the first time, I became seriously concerned for my own safety and that of my wife. You will now understand the paranoia to which I referred earlier."

"Do you still feel under threat?"

"Absolutely. I have come to realise that there are very powerful forces at play here and influences which go above and beyond my old company."

Declan was now taking a keen interest. "What about Glik, do you think he is behind all this?"

# Chapter 7 - Assault

The Professor sat back in his chair and paused to gather his thoughts. "In my experience, ambitious scientists fall into two categories. There are those who want fame, prizes, honours, global recognition, etc., and those who want money. You must know that even a small percentage of the patent rights to a blockbuster drug can be worth a fortune. Glik is a man who wants both. I am afraid that he is also a man who seems to stop at nothing to get what he wants. However, I now think there are even bigger forces at work. Glik is certainly a player, and an important one at that, but you need to look to the organisations which finance people like him."

Declan nodded. "Yes, I think our research has drawn us to a similar conclusion."

Another anaemic smile from Professor Lewis. "Mr Walsh gave me the bare bones of your situation over the telephone, but perhaps you could fill in some of the details, such as the name of this vaccine and who makes it. And why do you think Glik may be involved?"

It was time for Rob to take up the story." Apologies if I repeat facts you already know, but it might be worth giving you a comprehensive account from the beginning." He briefly related the past few weeks' events, starting with the visit to his surgery of young Julian Fellowes. He explained what little he had learned about the vaccine, "It is called Bercuvax, manufactured by ME Chemicals LLC, a Delaware-registered company with manufacturing facilities in Dubai. Its CEO is believed to be Professor Rafal Glik. As a Delaware company, we cannot trace the ownership. The local distributor in Kwandia is a company called Kwanpharm, which is registered in Dubai, so, again, we cannot trace its ownership. We cannot link Glik to that company, but otherwise, his name appears everywhere in this story."

The professor raised his eyebrows. "I am afraid I have never heard of ME Chemicals or Kwanpharm. I have never heard of Bercuvax either, but it is just a brand name. It is not uncommon for medications, including vaccines, to be marketed under different names, so you really need to identify its scientific definition, and it doesn't sound like the companies you have contacted are likely to provide that."

"What about MAGIC? Surely, they should be more helpful?"

Declan laughed. "With Glik as the chair of their key Policy and Programme Committee, I don't think we shall get very far there."

A nod of agreement from Professor Lewis. "I am afraid your friend is right."

"But if MAGIC is a global organisation aimed at improving world health by providing medication and vaccines to poorer countries, why would it withhold such information? It doesn't own commercial rights itself, does it?"

"No, but it does decide which medications it will back and often provides modest support to participating countries as in the Kwandian case. Remember that MAGIC was set up because other global bodies were considered too slow and bureaucratic in initiating medical programmes. However, it is much more commercially driven and has been criticised for effectively allowing private enterprises to determine world health objectives. Its market-oriented measures also result in medicines being sold at inflated prices to richer countries, whilst poorer countries are often priced out of the market altogether. You should also understand that MAGIC is funded not only by donations from Western governments but also from private donors, the largest of which is The Doorstep Foundation controlled by the philanthropist Jim Doors and his wife, Maddie."

Declan homed in immediately. "You mean the very same organisation which we believe is funding the project in Kwandia? A recipe for a conflict of interest if ever there was one!"

The professor was quick to acknowledge the point. "I am afraid that conflicts of interest are another criticism often levelled at MAGIC."

Declan laughed without humour. "What odds would you give me that ME Chemicals might happen to be owned by the benevolent Doorstep as well?"

Rob remained more cautious. "We don't actually know that."

"No, and we have no way of finding out for the present."

The two visitors felt that the meeting had reached a natural conclusion, and Professor Lewis was beginning to show signs of fatigue. They thanked him for the information he had provided, which had put some detail on the outline they had already established and confirmed their suspicions.

"Let me know when you have the lab tests back on the vaccine, and I may be able to shed more light on it. In the meantime, I will make some discreet enquiries among my contacts to see whether any of them have heard of this project. I have a lot of ears to a lot of grapevines."

Rob was concerned. "Please take care. We should hate to think that our visit may expose you to any danger."

***********************************

Driving back across the Sussex Downs, Rob was feeling downcast. It was in complete contrast to Declan, who had sped off in his sports car in an ebullient mood, having had all his suspicions confirmed and now felt he was on the trail of what could be a very big story.

The meeting filled in many of the gaps in their knowledge, but Rob was disturbed by some of the revelations about the big pharmaceutical companies and global entities such as MAGIC. They were important players in the medical universe, in which he also played a small part. He had never questioned their integrity or their motives. His mind went back to his upbringing in Africa and, in particular, to his mother. She was a fan of all things British, harboured no resentment towards them and had never regarded them as colonial masters. No longer part of an empire and having undergone a name change from Northern Rhodesia to Zambia, there remained a connection with Britain through membership of the Commonwealth. It made no difference to her since all she saw for her gifted son was an opportunity, so she pushed him hard through his academic studies and, ultimately, a university place in the mother country. When he qualified as a doctor from Cambridge, she was the proudest mother in Africa, if not the whole of the Commonwealth.

He also thought of Dr Fiesta in his battered old car, touring the villages and administering life-saving vaccines and other medicines. What would he have made of the information, or did he know? Rob was sure he had no idea.

His sombre mood continued all the way back to

London, where an empty house would greet him. Alice and the girls were still on vacation at her parents. It did nothing to improve his state of mind as he walked up the short path to his front door and began to fumble for his key.

He heard nothing and saw nothing, but he certainly felt it. By then, it was too late. The blow had been dealt expertly to the back of the cranium, and he collapsed in a heap like a sack of potatoes. It was followed by a foot aimed at his ribcage. He was sufficiently conscious to draw up his legs into the foetal position, hoping to ward off any further blows. But luck was on his side. At that very moment, his neighbour's front door opened as Roger Wilcox and his wife prepared to go out for the evening. The two assailants turned away at the sight of Roger and vanished into the street before he could even react.

"Good god, Rob! Whatever has happened? Are you alright? How badly are you hurt?" He and his wife made their way round to Rob's front path and helped him struggle to his feet. They opened his front door and helped him inside. Rob was slowly getting both his breath and his senses back now.
"Thanks. You appeared just in time. Did you get a look at them?"

"Not really. They both wore balaclavas. Both quite young, I think, but why on earth were they attacking you? We should call the police, and you need an ambulance."

Rob's mind was now back in gear and was trying to process his thoughts. He thought of Buster, Professor Lewis's dog and how the police had suddenly dropped the case. "No police at the moment, I think, and I'll be alright."

Roger frowned. "Surely a blow to the head should be treated immediately. You may have suffered a concussion."

"You are right, Roger, but I shall get myself looked at in the morning."

His neighbour shrugged his shoulders. "Well, you are the doctor, but why no police?"

Rob was thinking fast. "I think it may be drug-related. We had a break-in at the surgery last week, and some drugs were stolen. I need to check whether we have had any more disturbances there before calling the police. I will also do that in the morning as I can't face all that this evening."

Roger frowned again. Rob wasn't sure he had bought the explanation, but fortunately, his wife Patsy stepped in. "What you need is a good night's sleep. I know Alice and the girls are away. Is there anything we can get you or do for you?"

Rob smiled. "You are very kind, but I think your prescription is the right one, Patsy. I just need sleep."

They waved him a reluctant goodbye and saw themselves out. Rob immediately searched for his burner phone and punched in a text message to Declan. 'Urgent we meet. Lunch tomorrow. Usual place at 12.30 pm.'

# Chapter 8 - Sir Richard Prentice

Declan's usual sunny disposition disappeared rapidly as his friend described the events of the previous evening and the pain which he could still feel. His head ached slightly, and his ribs were still sore from the kicking.

"If Roger hadn't opened his front door when he did, I think they would have killed me, Dec."

The Irishman managed a smile. "Let me reassure you, my friend. If they had wanted to kill you, they would have done so. A knife in the ribs is quicker than either a blow to the head or a boot in the ribcage. These guys knew what they were doing."

Rob was not entirely convinced but had to accept the logic. "You mean that this was just a warning?"

"Exactly so. This is why we need to consider your future involvement in our escapade. You may not get off as lightly the next time. Your name is clearly out there, so I think you need to be withdrawn from the front line."

But Rob was not happy. The attack had brought home to him the seriousness of the situation, and his mind went back to the threats against Professor Lewis and the killing of his dog. He felt a shiver of fear run through his body. Nevertheless, he was not going to give up, and in some ways, the attack made him even more determined to expose the dangers of this vaccine.

"You mean we should give up?"

Declan leant forward and lowered his voice. "Not 'we'. I mean 'you'."

"So, what makes you think it is better for you to get beaten up than me?"

Another smile from Declan. "I am less at risk than you, being just a lowly journalist hack of the sort who is known for causing trouble and exaggerating everything, so who of importance will listen to me? You, on the other hand, are an eminent Harley Street physician whose word will carry some weight in medical circles. You are much more dangerous to them."

"Bollocks!" Dr Robson Ford was uncharacteristically blunt in his diagnosis. Declan was slightly taken aback but had to admit that his argument was pretty thin.

"I have come this far, and I am not about to be sidelined now, so what do we do next?"

"Well, one thing we can do is to debug your house and surgery. There is no point in pretending now that we have not found them, but at the same time, we don't want them listening in on your conversations. It will make our communication easier too. I will get Mackenzie to come round tomorrow morning."

Declan knew his friend, and he knew that he knew that he would not stop now. "Well, for the moment, we wait. We need to find out what this vaccine contains, so hopefully, you will hear from Julian's dad before long. In the meantime, I shall do a bit more digging into Kwandia as a country. It would be interesting to find out precisely why it was chosen by The Doorstep Foundation and Professor Glik for their programme."

Rob suddenly felt pleased with himself. "I am ahead of you. I have already set one bloodhound following that particular trail, so it will be interesting to see whether you both come up with the same story!"

\*\*\*\*\*\*\*\*\*\*\*\*\*\*\*\*\*\*\*\*\*\*\*\*\*\*\*\*\*\*\*\*\*\*\*\*

At about the same time as the two friends were meeting, another lunch was taking place in a different part of London and in different surroundings. Rob's father-in-law, Sir Richard Prentice, had for most of his career maintained membership of two gentlemen's clubs in London. One was not far from the Foreign Office in the St James's area and, therefore, useful for lunching with colleagues or parliamentarians. The other was the Caledonian Club, to which he had gained membership by using some distant Scottish ancestry to justify his entry. It was situated on the other side of Hyde Park Corner and was useful for those occasions when he wanted to avoid colleagues from his department or, at the very least, reduce the risk of running into them. This was one of those occasions.

His protégé, Sir Thomas Daltrey, had succeeded him as Permanent Under-Secretary and cut swiftly to the chase after exchanging the usual pleasantries. "What may I ask has sparked your interest in Kwandia? Is that where your son-in-law comes from?"

Sir Richard gave him an indulgent smile. "No, he is from Zambia, but as it happens, he is the reason I am here today. However, it is not strictly his African background that has prompted the inquiry; it is an incident arising from his medical practice. He has been treating a young patient who recently received a vaccine in Kwandia, which he believes is suspect. I don't know the details, but in trying to investigate its medical provenance, he has come up against a brick wall and believes there may be more to it than meets the eye. He asked me what I knew of the country, but I had to admit it was not very much. It rarely figured on our radar in my day."

"Well, not much has changed. According to Freddie Macer, who is head of our African desk, Kwandia is a small landlocked state with not a lot going for it. Extremely poor with a largely agricultural economy, although there are reputed to be some rare earth minerals in the west of the country. About a third of the country is desert. Historically, there have been the usual tribal rivalries, but these haven't surfaced in any meaningful way for a long time perhaps because the dominant religion is Islam and the majority of the population is Sunni Muslim although thankfully not of the extreme variety."

"Wasn't it a French colony originally, so presumably it is a Francophone nation."

"Yes and no. The President, Moussa Diaby, is English-educated. Went to Oxford as did the Finance Minister, Nouha Kyabou, though the latter also spent time in the States at Harvard Business School. English is now a major part of the school curriculum although, of course, that will only apply to the thirty percent of the population who actually attend schools."

"That must have put French noses out of joint."

Sir Thomas shrugged his shoulders. "Apparently, they aren't much bothered. The main concern of the Europeans and the Americans is keeping the Chinese out. One sniff of mineral deposits and the Chinese will be there, building roads, supplying medicines, etc. That brings me on to a further complication."

"Which is?"

It is rumoured that there is a growing rivalry between Kyabou and Diaby. The President is 'old school'. Rules with a rod of iron and likes to control everything. Though it has to be said, corruption is not as rife in Kwandia as in many African states. Kyabou, on the other hand, is very Americanised. Preaches democracy with a capital D, 'Will of the people', that sort of stuff. He goes down well with the younger element, of course, but there's no doubt that if he were to get power, he would be even more autocratic than the present incumbent."

Sir Richard nodded. "Well, we have seen that many times and not just in Africa. So, what is our position, that is if we have one?"

"Well, we have historically supported Diaby and continue to do so. There are a number of UK-based NGOs doing good work there. Water projects, constructing schools and that sort of thing. Diaby remains friendly to the West and has shown no inclination towards dealing with the Chinese. However, it is believed he recently received a high-level delegation from China, so it is a situation which we are monitoring. One must assume they are interested in the rare earth minerals.

"What about the Americans? Are they on the scene? I ask because the dodgy vaccine I mentioned appears to be a project backed by The Doorstep Foundation."

"You mean Jim Doors, the billionaire philanthropist?"

"The very same."

"Freddie made no mention of a vaccine programme or Doors. That is strange since we would normally be aware of a major project like that. And Doors is not one to hide his light under a bushel. He usually likes to go for maximum publicity. I will follow it up."

Sir Richard thanked his friend and looked forward to hearing any further information he might find out. However, in the taxi back to Victoria station, he reflected that he had not learned a great deal from the meeting and how very little substance he had to report to his son-in-law. Nevertheless, he would phone Rob in the evening and impart such little knowledge as he had gained. He might find the comments about Jim Doors interesting and that nothing appeared to be known about the vaccination project. He would also mention the mineral deposits and the fact that the president had recently received a Chinese delegation, although he could not see the relevance of either of these facts to the vaccination project.

# Chapter 9 - Simon Fellowes

A couple of days passed without incident. Rob thanked his father-in-law for his information, although he privately acknowledged that it had told him very little. He hoped Declan's digging would unearth rather more. Mackenzie had duly debugged both his surgery and his house, which somehow made him feel more comfortable, though in his heart of hearts, he knew he was probably even more vulnerable than before.

The news that he had been waiting for came in the form of a telephone call from Kate Fellowes. Her husband had arrived home and brought a sample case of twenty-four vaccine phials. He would deliver them to Rob's surgery the following morning if that were convenient.

Simon Fellowes was almost exactly as Rob had imagined him. Sandy-haired, softly spoken, with a slightly diffident manner. His skin was pale, and frankly, he did not look a picture of health. Rob had often noticed such features in white men who spent their lives in Africa and wondered why two weeks holiday in the Mediterranean gave their complexions a healthy glow whilst a lifetime under the burning heat of an African sun produced no tan at all. Alice had told him that lying on a holiday beach was one thing, but those who worked in the tropics spent their days avoiding the sun if they could and, wherever possible, sought the comfort of shade and, if they were lucky, an air-conditioned building. Rob thought she was probably right and remembered being taught that women in the Middle East often suffered from rickets caused by a deficiency of vitamin D, the so-called sun vitamin. Despite living in a sun-drenched climate, they were always covered from head to foot in clothing, often with veils and spent a large proportion of their time indoors.

His visitor carried an old shopping bag from which he produced a box containing the vaccines, which he placed on Rob's desk. Rob wanted to know how he had obtained them. He was pleased with Simon's answer.

"Well, when Kate told me that you had been fobbed off by the manufacturers, I thought that a straightforward request to the local project administrators might not be the way to go. Luckily, I have a good friend who is a district nurse covering the area around my headquarters, and she was able to oblige."

"So, no one knows you have taken some samples for testing."

"No one other than Mariam, and she will say nothing."

"Your wife told me that this vaccine project had diverted funds from your own charitable work in the country."

"Well, not too much in local funds since the vaccines have been supplied by an American foundation at what I understand to be a fraction of their normal price, but they have tied up local resources. Every government department is providing manpower, and nobody has time for anything else. In fact, I gained an audience with the President himself to complain about it."

"You know Diaby?"

"Very well. As it happens, my predecessor in the post was at Oxford with him, so our organisation has more or less got an open line to him."

"And what did he say?"

"He claimed to have very little knowledge of it. Said it was a project overseen by Nouha Kyabou, the Minister of Finance, but I sensed a little irritation in his voice."

Thinking back to the report from his father-in-law, Rob posed a question. "Does the President see Kyabou as a rival?"

Simon thought for a moment before replying. "Quite possibly. If Kyabou is behind this project, then it is quite a clever move on his part. A bit of one-upmanship, if you like. After all, the President can hardly be seen opposing a programme aimed at improving the nation's health as well as being financed by an American benefactor."

Rob sat back and pondered. "So long as it does improve the nation's health. He would not look so clever if it poisoned half the population. The sooner we can find out what is in this vaccine, the better."

The other man gave a rueful smile. "It's not the only thing worrying me at the moment."

Rob did his best to look sympathetic as Simon continued. "There has been a lot of geological surveying activity recently in the west of the country, and there are rumours of large deposits of spodumene
hard rock."

"Spodumene?" Rob had never heard of it.

"Apparently, it is the ore from which Lithium is extracted, and that mineral is becoming ever more valuable as a component in batteries for the expected boom in the manufacture of electric cars."

Rob was puzzled. "Surely that would be a good thing for the country, would it not?"

"Well, it depends on how much of the proceeds actually remain in the country, but that is not my main concern. According to some of my better-informed colleagues, lithium extraction presents significant environmental and health hazards, particularly in relation to water. It is known to cause water contamination, and even more worrying, the extraction process itself consumes massive amounts of water. I am told it is something like 1.9 million litres of water for every ton of lithium mined. That could be catastrophic in arid regions such as large parts of Kwandia."

Rob could now see Simon's concern. One of his major projects in Kwandia was devoted to bringing water and improved hygiene to the country, and here was an enterprise which seemed to be designed to do the opposite. He muttered words of sympathy and expressed the view that life was never easy, especially in Africa. However, he was impatient to progress testing on the vaccine now that he had some samples, and much as he understood Simon's predicament, he could not see how it could possibly connect with the vaccine project.

Before he left, Simon gave Rob detailed instructions on how to contact him in Kwandia should he have returned there before Rob had the results. Such guidance was necessary because his only internet access was a shared office computer, and the connection was rather unreliable. Mobile phone communication was equally patchy, especially from overseas. To overcome the lack of privacy and fickle connectivity, he had devised a protocol for contact with his wife, so Rob listened carefully to his instructions. He promised he would keep Simon fully in the picture.

**********************************

The following morning, Rob wasted no time contacting the private laboratory he had used in the past. He asked to be put through to his old friend Gordon. He decided to keep explanations to a minimum and merely stated in straightforward terms what he wanted and how soon he could expect the results.

His face fell when Gordon explained that analysing vaccines was a specialist activity that his lab had neither the equipment nor the expertise to carry out. "You will probably need to go to one of the big Pharma companies for that sort of thing." That was exactly what Rob did not want to do, and having put the phone down, he sat in his chair feeling somewhat despondent, trying to work out his next move. As usual, his next move was to phone Dec, who was also stumped for once and had no ready answer to this unexpected stumbling block. But Dec was nothing if not resourceful. "Leave it with me, but it might take a day or two."

Those were not comforting words for Rob, who felt that time was of the essence, but since he had no better ideas of his own, he was once again relying on his friend to find a way forward.

Dec, meanwhile, had an idea. He put out a call to Professor Owen Lewis. The Professor already knew the case's background and listened patiently to Declan's plea for help. After what seemed to Dec a very long silence, Professor Lewis spoke. "My old company had a small subsidiary with a laboratory near Cambridge, which would undoubtedly have the equipment and expertise you need." There was another long pause, but this time, Dec broke the silence. "If you can give me their name and contact details, I will get in touch right away."

"It may not be as easy as that. They work almost exclusively for companies and scientists within the group." There was another pause. "However, I still have a very good contact there who I know has done the odd private assignment from time to time. I will need to talk to him and come back to you."

Dec thanked him profusely and hoped that the professor's contact would play ball and that it would not take too long to arrange.

The professor came back to him the following day with the address of the laboratory and the name of his contact to whom the vaccine samples would need to be delivered personally. He had agreed to carry out the work for less than the normal charge, but it would need to be paid upfront and in cash. Dec quite understood. Best of all, from Dec's point of view, a rapid response was promised, which he understood to be no more than ten days.

Later that day, he collected the samples from Rob's surgery and explained to him where he would take them and when they could expect the results. He omitted any reference to Professor Lewis as he thought Rob might be concerned about exposing the professor to further risk. Rob had been given a box of forty phials, but, cautious as always, he decided to keep back twenty, giving the other half to Dec.

**********************************

Bouldham Laboratories Limited was presumably named after the remote village of Bouldham and the Business Park on which it was situated. Professor Lewis had described it as being 'near Cambridge', but it was more than halfway to Ely, and Dec found himself driving his bright red sports car more cautiously than usual across the flat open fenland. Many of the roads were quite narrow, and being higher than the surrounding fields, they fell away alarmingly on each side, often with wide water-filled ditches awaiting a reckless driver.

His satnav guided him to the small Bouldham Business Park, which was home to no more than a dozen establishments. He drove slowly through the main thoroughfare of the Park and observed that most of the buildings were warehouses or small production units. 'More like a Trading Estate than a Business Park', he thought to himself. It was not what he had expected, and neither was Bouldham Laboratories when he reached the last unit on the road. He had visited many pharmaceutical companies and Biotech laboratories in the course of his work and was more accustomed to modern premises with plenty of glass, stripped pine and shining marble foyers. Bouldham Laboratories did not fit that description. It was a brick, two-story building of roughly 1980s vintage, and the side windows he could see on the ground floor all had vertical steel bars for security. Nevertheless, some effort had been made to tart up the entrance, and the reception area had a smart wooden floor and some purple leather sofas of a sleek, modern design.

He walked across to the reception desk and asked for Mr Colin Redfearn. The young receptionist took his name, printed off a clip-on badge and asked him to take a seat. He began to leaf through one of the scientific journals on the coffee table in front of him but looked up from time to time as various staff members passed across the area and disappeared into one of the several doors leading off. Some wore smart navy tunics with light blue piping and the company logo stitched in the same colour. Others, mostly older staff, wore standard white laboratory coats which also displayed the company logo. Declan amused himself by guessing which uniform Mr Redfearn would favour and plumped for the white lab coat.

He had been waiting now for fifteen minutes and was beginning to become impatient. One of the doors to the side opened, and a man came out, but this time wearing a light brown coat more suited to a stockroom than a laboratory. He ignored Declan and walked briskly to the door right at the end, which was farthest from the entrance. As the door opened, Declan heard a shriek from within before it was firmly shut behind the man. His heart sank. He knew the call of a monkey when he heard one, and being an ardent anti-vivisectionist and fully paid-up member of an animal rights association, he was immediately distressed. Despite such beliefs, he was not a vegan or even a vegetarian. He enjoyed 'a good steak' and meat generally. His agile mind had enabled him to formulate an argument that many animals were natural carnivores and, after all, humans were also animals whose natural diet was omnivorous but most certainly would include meat. He convinced himself that one should never go against nature. Not only that, but he also asked himself, why would the Good Lord have equipped our mouths with canine teeth if he didn't want us to eat meat?

Whilst mulling over the pros and cons of his argument, he had sunk further back into the sumptuous armchair, and his eyelids were just beginning to descend when he became aware of a figure who had materialised silently in front of him. The man was wearing a white lab coat, so Dec inwardly congratulated himself on getting that right. He jumped to his feet.

Colin Redfearn was of medium height with a rather thin face and sharp, pointed features. He did not introduce himself, but when he spoke, it was with a cultured voice and an air of authority. "I take it that you are Owen Lewis's man and that you have something for me."

Declan did not care for the turn of phrase. He was

nobody's 'man' but decided to let it pass. After all, they were seeking a favour. "I am Declan Walsh, and I have indeed been referred by Professor Lewis. He handed over the box of vaccines to Redfearn together with a bulky white envelope containing the fee for carrying out the work in the form of a substantial number of £20 pound notes.

"Do I assume, Mr Walsh, that you have no medical or pharmaceutical qualifications?" It was more of a statement than a question. Declan pondered for a moment. "You assume correctly unless you count my science degree from Cambridge." The briefest of smiles flickered across Redfearn's face, but since he did not enquire further as to which branch of science he had studied, Declan accepted that his degree did not count.

"I shall report our findings to Professor Lewis only. He will be able to interpret them for your purposes, I am sure."

Declan was not best pleased with this response but had to accept it. "There is some urgency in this matter, so maybe I should leave my contact details with you just in case you cannot reach Professor Lewis." He kept two different business cards in his wallet. One contained his job title, email address and two telephone numbers. The other was a plain card with just his name and was useful for those occasions when he did not wish to disclose that he was a journalist. He chose the latter card and wrote his mobile number on the reverse before handing it to Redfearn.

"I expect to report our findings within seven days or sooner if possible."

Declan thanked him and returned to his car for the journey across the Fens and then back to London.

# Chapter 10 - Two Surprises

Declan had updated Rob with details of his Cambridge visit but omitted to tell him that they insisted on reporting to Professor Lewis. Rob was still in the dark about the Professor's role as the link to the laboratory, and Declan wanted to keep it that way. A sudden thought then crossed his mind. 'What if the Professor phoned Rob with the results? That would give his game away.'

He acted swiftly. A quick phone call was made to the Professor to report on his visit and thank him again for arranging it. He explained that Redfearn had insisted on reporting directly to him and apologised for putting him to more trouble. Would he then please contact only him with the results and not Rob 'as we need to keep communications within the smallest circle possible?'. He would, of course, share the findings with Rob, and they would need to decide on a course of action. Would the Professor wish to be kept informed of subsequent events, although he would understand if he wanted to distance himself from the affair.

The Professor said he did not wish to become more involved but would be interested to learn the outcome in due course. Declan was happy with this response.

Declan received a surprise call on his mobile two days after the visit. It was Professor Lewis, sounding slightly agitated. He had just received a call from Redfearn at the laboratory. They had already concluded their tests. "I wasn't sure whether Colin was pleased or irritated, but you need to prepare yourself for a surprise."

Declan said nothing but waited for the Professor to continue.

"The vaccine is no more than a weak saline solution. Pure water with a little salt and some baking soda. Perfectly harmless but unlikely to immunise you against TB."

*********************************

The following morning, Rob's first appointment was not until 11 o'clock, so he agreed to meet Declan for an early coffee to hear what his friend had described as 'puzzling and disturbing news'.

The coffee shop wasn't busy, and they had found a quiet table in the corner. Rob's frown grew ever deeper as he sipped his Americano and listened to his friend.

"It doesn't make sense. Why inject people with water? Is it just a massive financial fraud, and if so, who is defrauding whom? Who is benefitting? Is our friend Glik taking the Americans for a ride, or is it just the good people of Kwandia?"

Declan had been pondering the whole puzzle overnight and, therefore, had more time than his friend to consider the various possibilities. "Let's first go back to the beginning. Young Julian Fellowes presented at your surgery with what we now know to be TB, having received the vaccine the previous week. If it is completely harmless, why should that happen?"

Rob had an answer to that. "You have to remember that TB is rife in that country, and the most likely explanation is that he simply caught the disease from one of the locals. His parents were happy to let him play with the kids from the village in the mistaken belief he had been immunised."

Declan nodded. "So, a harmless vaccine isn't so harmless if it misleads people into thinking they have protection."

"Precisely."

"OK. I'll buy that explanation, but it still leaves a lot of questions unanswered."

"Well, as Professor Lewis said, can we be sure that the samples we tested were, in fact, the same vaccines as those administered to the locals?"

"Professor Lewis?"

Declan realised he had let the cat out of the bag. He was not overly worried as he expected his friend to find out sooner or later. Nevertheless, he managed to look suitably abashed.

"How does Professor Lewis fit into the picture?"

Rob's expression darkened as Declan explained that Professor Lewis had facilitated access to a suitable laboratory and darkened even more when he heard that the laboratory was owned by his former employer. He was inwardly angry with his friend but did not show it and made only one comment. "It was taking quite a chance, surely."

The discovery about the vaccine had shaken Declan, and Rob's remark brought home to him the risk he had taken but had not really thought too much about at the time. He began to regret having given Colin Redfearn his contact details. He brought his mind back to the present and what they should now do with the information. "We need to contact Simon Fellowes and inform him about the test results."

Rob shook his head. "Not yet. We must not put him in any danger, and this information could do precisely that. Ideally, as Professor Lewis said, we need to establish whether the samples we tested were not just dummies provided to put us off the scent."

"But how do we do that without contacting Simon?"

"Good question." Rob was thoughtful. "Simon obtained the samples from a district nurse who was actually administering them."

"Yes, Mariam."

"He seemed very confident that Mariam would not let on to anybody, so unless she has told one of her colleagues or is in league with the local vaccine suppliers, then let us assume for the moment that the samples are representative of the whole batch. What should we do then? Surely, we need to find out why. What is the purpose of such a scam, and who stands to gain?"

"You are right, Rob. We need to understand just what is going on here." Declan drained his coffee cup, and as he put it down, the ringtone on his mobile sprang into life. He glanced at the screen. There was a number he did not recognise, so he just terminated the call. Rob looked at him, but Declan shrugged his shoulders. "I only answer to numbers I know. If it is something important, they will leave a message." He was right, and this time, it was important. The message icon flashed up, and Declan rang the answerphone number.

"Hello, Mr Walsh. This is Colin Redfearn. I cannot reach Owen Lewis, but I have some further information you need to know about the tests we carried out. Please telephone me on this number as a matter of urgency."

Declan wasted no time but rang back immediately, with Rob looking on attentively. Redfearn's voice was almost a whisper, and he seemed agitated. "I must apologise," Declan said nothing. "I'm afraid we missed something. My assistant started to pour away the vaccines when he noticed what he thought was a speck of dust. He looked more closely at the other phials and found they all contained the same specks. Under a microscope, it can be seen that they are miniature microchips no more than 0.1 cubic millimetres in size. I believe computer scientists refer to them as 'motes'. I have read somewhere that such chips are injectable."

Declan was astonished. "Can you tell what the chip contains?"

"Afraid not. Our laboratory is equipped for chemical analysis, but this will need a very different technology. What do you want me to do with the vaccine phials? Will you collect them?"

Declan knew that Rob had kept back half of the sample bought over by Simon, a decision which now looked very wise in hindsight. "Would you mind hanging on to them for the time being as we have further samples we can use. If you don't hear from me in two weeks, you can destroy them."

He thanked Redfearn and rang off.

Rob had picked up the gist of the conversation. He slumped back in his chair and stared at his friend in amazement. Whatever the two men were expecting to find in the vaccine, they were unprepared for this. He gave a hollow laugh. "What the hell does it mean?"

Declan's brain was already in overdrive. "What it means, my friend, is that we have stumbled on something here that we shouldn't have."

"And what exactly is it we have stumbled upon?"

"At the moment, I haven't the faintest idea, but I am pretty sure it is not just medical. That is just a cover. This could also be financial or political or perhaps both."

"And dangerous?" Rob posed the question casually.

"Potentially very dangerous, which is why you were beaten up."

"So, what do we do now?

Declan uttered just one word, "Mackenzie."

"You think he can help?"

"He's the best I can think of. Or rather his company. Micro-computers should be up their street. After all, their business is cyber security, corporate espionage, etc. If they can't actually read what is on these microchips, they might at least give us some clues as to what they could be used for. I suggest I come back with you to your surgery and pick up some more of the phials. Then, I'll take them straight round to Mackenzie."

"And Simon. I suppose we say nothing to him until we have more to go on?"

"Absolutely. We need to give him a full story so he can act quickly when the time is right. Anything less could expose him to danger if he starts asking questions of the wrong people. At the moment, his role in passing us the vaccine samples is unknown to anyone except ourselves."

When Declan had gone, Rob was glad to get back to work and turn his mind to his patients' relatively straightforward medical problems. Finally, when the last patient had gone, he sat in his surgery chair, reflecting on the discoveries made by the laboratory and shaking his head in disbelief. As he walked home that evening, he weighed in his mind how much he should tell Alice about the latest turn of events. It was vital to keep their knowledge to themselves at this juncture. Any leak could be dangerous.

However, when he got home and slumped in his armchair with a restorative whisky, Alice noticed his unusually pensive mood and enquired what was troubling him. He could not bottle it up and gave her the latest update on the vaccine saga, as she called it. She was astonished and equally puzzled at what it all meant. Rob gave her Declan's take on it with a stern warning that she must not breathe a word to a living soul.

"I will not mention to anyone, not even to Daddy."

Rob sat up abruptly. "Especially not to him!"

He relaxed back into his chair. "Declan said that Mackenzie's people would take at least a week to come up with their findings so we can plan something for next weekend without any more shocks to the system.

Unfortunately, he was wrong.

# Chapter 11 - Suicide

It was lunchtime, and Mary had brought back his favourite crayfish and rocket sandwich from Pret for him. He was eating it and at the same time studying the case notes in preparation for his first patient that afternoon when there was a ping on his mobile phone announcing a message. It was a simple one-liner from Declan. 'Look at the breaking news and ring me immediately.'

Like many people, it had been a long time since Rob had bought a newspaper, and these days, he didn't even watch the News on terrestrial television. Instead, he relied on a news app on his mobile phone, which he now opened and scrolled down through. Such was the cryptic nature of his friend's message that he was not at all sure what he was looking for. He hoped for the best, but his mind feared the worst. His mind won.

After scrolling through a number of items, there it was. The headline hit him between the eyes. 'Professor found dead in 'Virginia Woolf' suicide'.

He read slowly through the piece. 'The body of Professor Owen Lewis, 74, a former Head of Research at one of the country's largest pharmaceutical companies, was found yesterday in the River Ouse in Sussex in what the police described as a bizarre reenactment of the suicide of Virginia Woolf seventy-six years ago. Professor Lewis was wearing a raincoat, the pockets of which were filled with stones to weigh him down in an identical fashion to Virginia Woolf in 1941. Although her body had been washed along the river and found three weeks later about a thousand yards away, it is known from footprints and the discovery of her walking stick that she entered the water near the village of Rodmell, where she lived. Professor Lewis, also a resident of Rodmell, was found at almost exactly that same location. He was known to be an admirer of Virginia Woolf's writing and often acted as a volunteer on days when Monk's House, her home in the village, was open to the public. It is now a National Trust property. Unlike her, though, it is believed he left no suicide note. Police have stated that they do not suspect foul play but at the same time are keeping an open mind.'

Rob scrolled back to the start and read the report again, slowly evaluating every word as he went. This was partly to make sure he had not missed anything but also to try and calm himself down as his mind was racing in several directions at once. He had two overriding thoughts. Firstly guilt. He was sure that the Professor's death was connected to their investigation, and he was inwardly cursing Declan for involving him in the laboratory testing. Secondly, was it suicide, or was he murdered? It appeared to be an elaborately staged reconstruction of a suicide which happened seventy-six years ago, and he could not make up his mind whether this favoured one theory or the other. Would an assassin go to all that trouble, and would they know of his appreciation of Virginia Woolf and his involvement with Monk's House?

On the other hand, why would a suicide use such a method? The professor had an interest in Virginia Woolf and her writings, but so far as he knew, it was purely academic and by no means an obsession. But he left no note. For Rob, that was the clincher. The more he thought about it, the more convinced he became that this was no suicide.

The question then became what to do now. He wanted to think things through before phoning Declan. There would need to be further police investigation, but judging by the quote in the report, their mind was already made up. He remembered the tale of Buster the Lewis's dog and how the police appeared to close down the case with unseemly haste. He expected a repeat performance here, which would also be the same for the coroner's inquest. He would also need to contact Mrs Lewis, although that was not a conversation he was looking forward to.

He needed more information and still had many questions. It was time to phone Declan.
His friend had already come to the same conclusion as himself and wasted no time letting him know. "It was murder. I feel it in my bones. Lewis did not strike me as the type to commit suicide, but if he had decided to take his own life, he was most definitely the type to have left a note explaining why, and there was no note, according to that

report."

At the other end of the phone, Rob was nodding in agreement. "I am sure you are right, but what do you make of the 'Virginia Woolf' set up? Why do that?"

"Good question. I think it was done to emphasise the suicide angle. To have just found him in the water might have aroused suspicions. But it tells us that they must have built up quite a knowledge of Lewis over time to have been able to link him in any way with the Virginia Woolf story. What do we do now?"

"First, we must contact Mrs Lewis, although not just to offer our condolences. We need to get her opinion about the suicide. After all, he may have been suffering from depression, which we didn't know about."

"Do you think she will blame us in any way?"

Rob grimaced. "I am afraid she will if she thinks it's murder. Why else would someone want to kill him?" It was a comment that did nothing to allay Declan's guilt over using the Professor to get the samples tested.

The two men continued to discuss their next move and, in particular, who should contact Mrs Lewis. As the medical practitioner, it was decided Rob would be the best suited to the task. Declan was relieved to be let off the hook. "But I think you should wait until tomorrow, Rob. She might still be in a state of shock."

"I have a busy day tomorrow. I probably won't be free until late afternoon. I have a patient at 2 pm, a bigwig in the city who just happens to be one of Alice's senior directors. It appears he trod on something nasty on holiday in the Caribbean, and his foot has swollen up like a football."

"Well, I am due to see Mackenzie tomorrow morning, so why don't I drop round to your surgery at, say, four o'clock, and Mary can make me a nice cup of tea? You can make your phone call, and I can update you on what Mackenzie might have found out. How does that sound?"

"Hopefully, I should be clear by then. If not, you will have to wait and talk to Mary."

"Well, that'll be no hardship, but I thought the average appointment with a medical practitioner lasted no more than ten minutes, fifteen at the most."

Rob smiled. "Not if you are a city tycoon and you or your medical insurance is paying my fee."

He could hear Declan groan. "See you tomorrow then."

**********************************

Walking home that evening, Rob was turning over in his mind what he should tell Alice, if anything, about Professor Lewis. He decided it was best to say something because she would almost certainly pick it up from the news, and then she would wonder why he had not mentioned it. That might make her worry more. In any event, she was already ahead of him.

"Wasn't it a Professor Lewis you went to see when we were staying down in Sussex?"

"Yes, it was, and I have seen the news." Rob tried to sound as deadpan as possible.

"Rather an unusual way to commit suicide, wasn't it? They don't seem to have any idea why he did it."

Rob said nothing. He had just stopped himself from saying, 'That's if it was suicide.'. But Alice continued, "They said he was an admirer of Virginia Woolf's writing, but even so, copying her suicide seems extreme, to say the least. Rob felt more uncomfortable, especially when she asked a very awkward question.

"I hope it had nothing to do with your visit."

He paused before answering. He had not told her of Professor Lewis's involvement in arranging the test and was certainly not going to mention his suspicions about his death. "I shouldn't think so.

I got the impression that he had quite a lot on his mind, and I really have no idea what his general health was like. There could be many reasons, but I agree with you that the Virginia Woolf thing is certainly bizarre."

It was now Alice who went quiet. She could read her husband pretty well. It was not so much what he said but the measured tone of his voice which caused her concern. She felt sure he was not telling her everything, but she hoped she was worrying unnecessarily. She decided to change the subject.

"I gather Ted Archer is coming to see you tomorrow."

"Yes, I will have the pleasure of meeting Sir Edward. Shall I ask him for some financial tips?"

# Chapter 12 - An Awkward Conversation

Declan arrived promptly at four o'clock as arranged, but Rob was still with his patient, and his door was firmly closed. This allowed him to turn on his charm for Mary, and they chatted amiably for about twenty minutes. This was no hardship for Declan, but pleasant though he found her company, it was not what he had come for, and he began to get impatient. "Sir Edward Archer is certainly getting his money's worth."

Mary smiled indulgently. "Actually, he arrived about half an hour late, so I am afraid you may have to wait a little longer."

Almost on cue, the surgery door opened, and a well-fed-looking man in his fifties wearing a Saville Row suit hobbled out. He gave Declan a curt nod of acknowledgement before turning to Mary. "Goodbye, nurse, and thank you."

When he had gone, Rob appeared at the doorway and motioned Declan to come in and join him. "No calls, Mary, just take messages."

"I'll say you are with a patient." To her surprise, Rob's face lightened up. "Yes, say that if you like, but I wouldn't have him as a patient. Mary feigned surprise. "Why not?"
"Well, he's incurable!" He laughed at his own joke, and Declan forced a grin. Mary was pleased to see

her doctor in such a relaxed state of mind. Ever since young Julian Fellowes had set foot in the surgery, his mood had become unusually sombre and, at times, clearly stressed. She put down his better humour to the arrival of Declan.

However, when the two men disappeared into the consulting room, his serious demeanour returned, and he now had to face making the phone call he had been secretly dreading.

The ringtone continued for what seemed an eternity before a voice answered. It was the same cut-glass voice as Mrs Lewis but just enough of a difference for him to know it was not her. "I wonder if I might speak to Mrs Lewis, please?" Rob tried to find the right balance between deferential and authoritative if such a balance could be found.

"I am sorry, but Mrs Lewis is not available at the moment." The enunciation of the words was crisp and self-assured. Rob asked with whom he was speaking but felt he knew the answer. He was right. "I am Margaret's sister, Ellen." She gave no further information and did not inquire who was speaking. The phone went silent.

"My name is Doctor Ford, and I have recently had some dealings with Professor Lewis on an important matter. Firstly, I should like to offer my condolences to Mrs Lewis, er Margaret and your family for your very sad loss. I quite understand that she must still be in a state of shock. I have no wish to intrude upon your grief, but please believe me when I say it really is essential that I speak to her as a matter of urgency. Perhaps you would be kind enough to pass on my message and ask her to call me when she feels up to it."

There was another pause. "I will pass on your message, Doctor. You had better leave me your telephone number." Rob duly spelled out the number, which he was asked to repeat, and finally rang off.

He got up from his chair, took a deep breath and walked to the door. "Mary, if a Mrs Lewis should ring, please put her straight through." Mary nodded, and he returned to sit down with Declan.

"Well, what did our friend Mackenzie have to say?"

Declan took some papers out of his document case and grinned broadly. "Mr Mackenzie was very excited, just like the proverbial dog with two tails! It appears that every corporation on the planet is trying to create the world's smallest computer chip, not to mention the research scientists at all the major universities, sometimes in collaboration with those corporations who presumably provide the funding. Mackenzie and his people knew all about them because they had been tracking the research but had never seen one before. However, this is where it gets complicated. They confirmed that the tiny specks in our vaccine samples were indeed microcomputer chips, but without an appropriate scanner or sensor, there is no way of knowing what data it contains or if it contains any data at all."

Rob was puzzled. "What do you mean?"

"Well, we still have no idea as to its purpose. There might well be a second phase in the process which is needed to load data onto it."

Rob was about to ask another question when the telephone rang. Mary's Scottish tones were clear and precise, "Mrs Lewis on the phone for you."

"Mrs Lewis, thank you so much for calling back. I am very sorry to trouble you at a time like this. May I first offer you my sincere condolences on what must have been a dreadful shock for you?"

There was a short pause before the words came out. Delivered in those cultured tones, they seemed even more jarring to Rob's ear. "The bastards got him in the end!"

That short outburst told him all he needed to know. "Are you saying that he did not commit suicide?"

Her voice was emotional as she sought to control her anger. "There is no way Owen would have contemplated suicide, Dr Ford. I am convinced he was murdered."

"I see. What do the police say?"

"Hah, the police are as good as useless. There is no way we are going to get a proper investigation. They want the case closed as quickly as possible."

It confirmed Rob's worst fears. "But there will need to be a coroner's inquest."

"That will be the same, I'm afraid. It will be a complete whitewash. I am sure of it."

There was a question Rob had to ask, but he was almost afraid to do so. "If you believe he was murdered, can you tell me why?"

The reply was swift. "I was hoping you might be able to tell me that, Dr Ford."

"You believe it may have been connected to our visit?"

"Well, that and the subsequent testing he arranged for your colleague."

The last comment hit home with Rob, and his sense of guilt returned, as did his suppressed anger with Declan, who was sitting opposite him at the table, trying to catch the drift of the conversation. "If that is the case, I can only offer you our sincere regrets. Please believe me that there is no way we would have knowingly exposed your husband to risk. Frankly, we have only recently become aware of the dangers inherent in our investigation."

When Margaret Lewis spoke again, Rob detected a slight softening in her tone. "I appreciate your comments, Doctor Ford, and if it is any comfort, I cannot be certain that it was your investigation which triggered his murder. Owen had his fingers in lots of pies and connections with many people dedicated to exposing corruption in the pharmaceutical world. I have known for some time that he was at risk, so in reality, any one of those cases could have been the cause. It is just that you were his most recent contact."

Rob did not know what more he could add, but Mrs Owen continued with a warning. "Of course, if it is your affair which was the cause, then you and your colleague may well be in danger. You must take extra precautions, and so must your families." The last words sent a chill through his spine.

"I assume that his funeral will not be for some time unless, of course, they fast-track the inquest."

He was surprised by her reply. "There will be no funeral, at least not in the customary sense of the word, so the inquest will not interfere with our plans."

"I'm sorry, I am not sure I understand."

"My husband was a scientist and liked to think that in life he was rational and realistic; matter of fact if you like. He wished his death to be likewise. He abhorred all forms of ritual and left strict instructions in his will that he should be cremated without ceremony, not even close family or friends attending. Thus, whenever his body is released, it will be collected and disposed of in the most efficient way possible. There are companies which specialise in this."

The certainty with which she spoke suggested to Rob that Mrs Lewis shared her husband's beliefs.

But she continued. "However, I know that a number of his friends and contacts are planning to hold a 'gathering' in central London in honour of his memory. I shall, of course, be there, and I believe you would find many of his contacts interesting and possibly helpful in aiding your investigation. I will let you know the time and place when I know the details. You and Mr Walsh will be most welcome. It is likely to be within the next two weeks."

Rob thanked her and confirmed his telephone number before ringing off.

Declan had followed most of the conversation but had not caught the last part. When Rob explained the chance to meet the professor's contacts, he became quite animated. "Could be just the opportunity we need. I am sure there will be some interesting characters amongst his acquaintances."

Rob sat back in his chair, relieved to have got the telephone call out of the way. He called for Mary to bring two cups of tea and told her she might as well go home. Then he turned back to Declan.

"Now, what were you saying about microchips?"

# Chapter 13 - Microchips

Declan picked up the papers he had taken out of his document case and, with a flourish, fanned them out like a conjurer with a pack of cards. He lifted out one of them and laid it out on the table. It was a sheet of A4 paper to which was sellotaped what appeared to be a press cutting. "Exhibit One!" he pronounced grandly.

Rob looked at the paper and shrugged his shoulders. "Very impressive, I'm sure, but it's all in Chinese."

"Korean, actually, but if you care to turn it over, there is a translation on the back."

Rob took some time to read it through before bursting out laughing. The press cutting was from a specialist law journal and headed up 'Neurotechnology and the Law'. It described the invention of a small microchip which could be inserted into the brain and was being developed by a joint venture between a Korean electronics company and an American multinational. The idea was to load up the embedded chip with years of case law and precedents, which the 'bionic lawyer' could access in a fraction of the time it would normally take them to read through by conventional means, thus saving their clients the costs of hours of billable time. It could transform the legal profession.

Rob read it through again, and the grin on his face

grew broader. "So, what are you suggesting, Dec? Is this a grand project to convert the whole of the Kwandian population into corporate lawyers and launch them on the world to undercut the major US and international firms and their extortionate fees?"

Dec had to laugh. "No, you fool. As I said at the outset, I don't know the objective of the project in Kwandia, but this information from Mackenzie tells us what is out there now and may give us a clue as to what they are doing. Take this example, for instance. If you can implant masses of legal stuff into someone, what other data could be implanted?"

It was a fair point which Rob had to concede. "What else have you got?"

Another flourish from Dec. "Exhibit Two!"

He pushed more paper across the table. This time, it was a longer article, two pages stapled together. Rob began to read, but Declan could not resist providing his own commentary. "This is probably more up your street since it is effectively a medical device being developed by scientists at a top American University. The microchip is implanted into the body and collects data such as temperature, blood pressure, etc, but the boffins believe it can be developed to detect disease and infections, even tumours. Imagine that as a cheap and rapid diagnostic tool."

"So, now you are going to replace doctors?" Rob was smiling again. "First lawyers and then doctors. The learned professions will disappear and be replaced by microchips!"

"Well, not yet. There are a few practical issues relating to number two. Currently, you need an ultrasound machine to read the data stored on the microchip, which must limit its usefulness. Furthermore, the methodology has so far been tested only on laboratory rats. It has some way to go before it can be used on humans."

Rob leaned back. "So, not likely to be a starter then."

"I hope not."

"What do you mean, you hope not?"

Declan became serious. "Remember our conversation with Professor Lewis. He reminded us of the number of times African populations, particularly in the small, poorer countries, had been used for testing new drugs and medical procedures that were still experimental. Well, let's suppose someone has been able to develop this technology further along the road than the geeks in their University laboratory. Who would be better able to learn of such a development than our friend Glik, with all his contacts through the MAGIC organisation? And who would have enough money to finance such a trial? Step forward Jim Doors and his

Doorstep Foundation."

"Surely not?" Rob was aghast. "The risks are enormous, and they would need local cooperation."

"Fairly easily bought, I imagine. But think back to something Simon Fellowes told us. He said President Diaby seemed only vaguely aware of the vaccine project and that the driving force behind it in Kwandia was the Finance Minister, Nouha Kyabou. And didn't your father-in-law say there was a hint of rivalry between those two? I see a bigger picture emerging here even if I cannot yet join the dots."

Rob was thoughtful. "You may be right about a bigger picture, but I am not convinced that Exhibit Two plays a role. What else have you got in your bag of tricks?"

The papers were shuffled again, and Declan laid out another sheet of A4 paper, which was a printout from an online magazine article. It was headed 'The world's smallest computer, no bigger than a grain of salt'. The report went on to describe an invention by a US multinational corporation in the electronics industry. However, the microprocessor was designed to be inserted in products rather than people and used to securely track goods in the global supply chain to prevent fraud.

Rob could not immediately see the relevance of this to the Kwandian project.

"Read on, young man." Declan was looking smug. "I will save you the trouble. This tiny chip is designed to work alongside blockchain technology."

"Blockchain?" Like many people, Rob had heard the word but really had very little idea of what it did and how it worked.

"Yes, Blockchain. Without getting too technical, Blockchain is like a massive digital database or ledger where the information is stored in blocks linked together via cryptography, and that, once stored, the history of those transactions is irreversible."

"You are already getting too technical." Rob frowned.

"Well, ignore the technology. You just need to understand that one of the biggest applications of Blockchain is the creation of cryptocurrencies such as Bitcoin. Supposing someone has found a way of inserting these chips into people loaded with financial data, giving them access to currency and payment systems. Like having an implanted credit card."

Rob was still frowning. It all seemed rather fanciful to him.

But Dec was not to be put off. He proudly produced yet another sheet of paper, "Exhibit Four!"

As he read it, Rob burst into laughter. Each idea seemed more implausible than the last, and this one was the most bizarre of all. A Californian company had invented a microchip that could be injected between the thumb and index finger and scanned and read by a mobile phone. According to the company's chief executive, the chip was designed to replace a business card and would turn the holder into 'some kind of cyborg'.

"So, before they loaded themselves up with legal precedents to undercut the international corporate legal firms, the good people of Kwandia would first roam the world waving their digital business cards to drum up trade." Rob was almost in hysterics.

Even Dec could now see the funny side, but he was not to be deterred. "You may laugh, but I am not interested in business cards. Try to imagine other applications for that technology. Look, I don't think any of the examples I have shown you are the precise answer to our problem, but what they show is just how much is out there. The four items I have selected are no more than a small sample. Just suppose our friends at the Doorstep Foundation had got their hands on a similar microchip? Who knows what they might be up to?"

Rob had to acknowledge that his friend was right. "It is undeniable that these chips are being inserted into the arms of the population of Kwandia. All we have to do is find out why."

His friend suddenly sprang to life. "Say that again!"

"What do you mean?

"Just repeat what you said."

Rob repeated his words.

"You said 'inserted into their arms'. Are we sure about that? Remember, some of those examples had them inserted into brains, hands, and who knows where."

Rob picked up the phone and began punching in numbers.

"Who are you phoning?"

"Well, there is only one way to find out. I am going to ask the recipient of the vaccine."

When Kate Fellowes answered, Rob was quick to ask after young Julian and was glad to hear he was almost back to his normal self. He asked whether the boy was there and, if so, whether he might have a word with him. Kate was puzzled by the request but called out to her son to come to the phone. Putting on what Mary called his best bedside manner voice, he said he was glad to hear that he was well on the way to a full recovery.

"Thank you, Doctor," came the polite reply.

"Now, Julian, I want you to think back to when you had the vaccine injection. Can you remember that?"

"Yes."

"Good. Now, can you tell me where on your body they injected you?"

"It was in my left arm, just below the shoulder."

"Thank you so much, Julian. You have been most helpful. That was all I really wanted to know."

But Julian had not finished. "I don't know whether it is important, but I noticed I was the only one who had the injection in the arm. The others were all injected in their hands between the thumb and big finger. The nurse was going to do mine in the same place, but a senior doctor was visiting that day, and he told the nurse to put mine in the arm. He said something about me being a European, and we react differently."

The boy's statement took Rob aback, but Declan was now looking smug.

"Business cards." was all Declan said, with a big grin on his face.

# Chapter 14 - Nouha Kyabou

Like other small African states, the People's Republic of Kwandia did not possess a flagship airline of its own. There was no Air Kwandia or Kwandair, but the country did have a central airport which went by the grandiose title of Diaby International Airport, named after its long-serving President. The airport was mostly served by a handful of other African airlines, but some truly international flights touched down there on a regular basis. One such was Air France, which operated a scheduled return flight to Paris four times a week.

It was in business class on one of their flights that the Minister of Finance, Nouha Kyabou, sat with his favourite wife, Oumou, embarking on what his staff and colleagues had been told was a well-deserved city break for no more than a couple of nights. There was no first-class cabin for this service, so the minister and his wife had to make do with business class. Nevertheless, it did not detract from their state of contentment as they sipped a glass of champagne before take-off. Champagne was not readily available in Kwandia and prohibited for Muslims, but this 'minor' transgression only added to their pleasure. As it happened, each of them had entirely different reasons for their satisfied smiles as the plane taxied out onto the runway.

For Oumou, it was indeed going to be a short vacation. Even if it amounted to little more than a whole day in Paris, it would be a whole day devoted to one of her favourite activities, shopping. She had planned her visit carefully, and as she relaxed in her seat, she rehearsed her itinerary in her mind. Having spent three years as a medical student at the Sorbonne in her youth, she knew Paris well. She remembered the most fashionable and luxurious streets which she had often visited as an impoverished student just to look and 'lick the steam from the windows' as her friend Della used to say. But now things would be different. She had access to the Ministerial credit card and would be unencumbered by a husband who would be tied up all day 'on business'. Small wonder she was grinning from ear to ear.

They were staying at the Hotel George V on the Avenue of that name just off the Champs Elysees. It was one of a handful of Parisian hotels classified as 'Distinction Palace' hotels, which carried an official government rating considered to be above five stars. Its restaurant had no fewer than three Michelin stars. It was a pity they would have to entertain their local Consul-General and his wife tonight. He was a pleasant enough little man but someone she regarded as a typical civil servant, and a dull evening lay ahead. She consoled herself by supposing it was a small price to pay for tomorrow's pleasures, so her mind readily returned to her plans.

She would start in the morning by strolling down the Champs Elysees just to see what was on offer there these days, but her real target was the

Rue du Faubourg Saint-Honore. Geographically, it was a rather narrow and undistinguished street compared with the grand boulevards laid out by Baron Haussmann in the middle of the nineteenth century, but it housed some of the most important buildings in Paris and the most fashionable. On one side were the Elysee Palace, the official residence of the French President, as well as the American and British embassies. But it was mostly the other side of the road which interested Oumou. Every major fashion house worth its salt was represented by a flagship store. This was the place for the very latest in clothing, handbags, shoes and jewellery. Despite their brand names, she remembered the shops themselves were rather modest in size, and the window displays classy but not extravagant. Of course, they contained nothing so vulgar as price tags. She knew only too well that if you needed to ask the price, you couldn't afford to shop there.

She would then have a light lunch at Laduree. The original patisserie shop, of course, was in the Rue Royale, not one of the branches that had now sprung up all over the place, including abroad. She would probably just order a salade nicoise followed by a couple of their world-famous macarons. That would keep her going before she tackled the 'grands magasins' in the Boulevard Haussmann.

She wondered what they were like these days and remembered a conversation with an Egyptian woman at an official cocktail party two years ago who told her of a recent visit she had made to Au

Printemps. Apparently, every shop assistant on the ground floor had been Chinese. 'All of them young, slim and attractive,' the woman had said. 'And about 75 per cent of the customers were also Chinese. It was like shopping in Beijing.'

Oumou reflected on that conversation. The Chinese seem to get everywhere these days. Only a week ago, she had seen a whole bunch of them in Kwandia. They appeared to have come from one of the government buildings in the city centre. She had mentioned it to her husband but afterwards wished she had not. He had reacted angrily and walked away.

But he was not angry now. In fact, quite the reverse. His face wore a similar contented smile to hers, although for very different reasons. Several times throughout the flight, she would notice him patting the jacket of his suit covering the inside breast pocket. It seemed to be an act of reassurance to confirm that the pocket's contents were still in place. She was right, although she had no idea what he was carrying. In fact, there were two white envelopes, and each time he touched them, a satisfied smile crossed his face.

When they left the arrivals hall, they quickly spotted the man holding a board with their names, and they followed him out of the building to a waiting car at the curbside, which the hotel concierge service had provided. It was a black Peugeot with plush leather seats and all the usual trimmings of a luxury saloon.

Nevertheless, the Minister would have preferred a Mercedes and hoped that standards at the Hotel George V were not slipping. He was only partly mollified by the driver's explanation that Peugeot had been the supplier of official cars to every French President since 'the beginning of time'.

\*\*\*\*\*\*\*\*\*\*\*\*\*\*\*\*\*\*\*\*\*\*\*\*\*\*\*\*\*\*\*\*\*\*\*\*\*\*\*\*

The following morning, they had a very early breakfast sent up to their suite. The Minister left his wife well before the shops would be open and made his way down to the hotel entrance. The black Peugeot was waiting for him, parked on the service road in front of the hotel. It would now make the reverse journey to their arrival yesterday and drew up at Charles de Gaulle airport in plenty of time for him to catch the first scheduled Swissair flight to Zurich.

At Zurich, he was met by Dr Eric Kraft, a senior attorney with one of the oldest law firms in the Canton of Zug, to which they were now headed in Dr Kraft's white BMW. The drive took about an hour, during which time the Minister reflected on his mission and congratulated himself on being a clever man. He believed he had judged the transaction perfectly. Less intelligent men might well have been too greedy, but he was proceeding with caution. Yes, there were some instant financial benefits to himself, but it was political gain that was his ultimate goal. The really big financial rewards would then follow.

For this reason, he had chosen to come to Zug, where Dr Kraft was going to set up a 'Verein' for him, a form of trust peculiar to Switzerland that had a number of advantages for his purposes. Chief of which was the absence of any form of registration and the minimum of paperwork needed to set it up. This meant it would be largely hidden from sight but, at the same time, could be presented to third parties when necessary as a perfectly legitimate organisation. After all, many large International bodies and NGOs were constituted as vereins, such as the World Wildlife Fund, Amnesty International and even the international football federation FIFA. Of course, the simplicity of its structure had another important benefit for the Minister. It only needed two directors, and these directors would have complete control over its assets.

More than once during the journey, the thought of the Swiss legal system brought a satisfied smile to his face and caused him to pat the breast pocket of his suit. The two envelopes were still there.

Zug was not only the name of a canton or district in Switzerland but also the name of its principal town. Dr Kraft's law firm was in an old building recently modernised along a main road in the town centre. Having settled themselves in his office with coffee and cakes, they immediately got down to business. Dr Kraft produced a small sheaf of documents that had been largely prepared in advance and that, the Minister noted, were headed Citizens of Kwandia Trust. The name had been his idea. A document containing several pages of closely typed German was handed to him, together with a French transcript. Dr Kraft explained that these were the statutes of the Verein if the Minister wished to study them. He spent a few minutes glancing through the French version and nodded his approval. The attorney then produced some further papers for signature, which appointed both Minister Kyabou and Dr Kraft as directors. Effectively, the two men could not only manage all operations of the Trust, but they also controlled all of its assets.

Dealing with the paperwork took little more than half an hour, and the Minister was impressed with the efficiency of his Swiss lawyer. The latter got to his feet. "If you do not mind a very short walk across the road, we can now proceed to our next appointment."

The two men walked for a couple of blocks before crossing the road and entering a rather more modern building with the name Baumgarten AG, Private Bank, in such discreet lettering it was hardly visible to passers-by. But then passers-by were unlikely to form the basis of this bank's clientele, which also stated underneath its name that it had been formed in 1922. In fact, this made it a relative youngster in Swiss banking terms, some of its peers being able to trace their origins back to the eighteenth century.

A smartly dressed young man introduced himself as

Wolfgang Lerner and led them from the reception area down a short corridor into a private office with glass walls on two of the sides. They accepted the offer of more coffee, which also came accompanied by some cookies. The Minister judged Herr Lerner to be smart not only in appearance but also in every other respect, and he was glad that Dr Kraft had insisted on accompanying him to open the bank accounts. "I can personally recommend this bank," he had said, "but even so, it is never wise for a client to deal directly with a banker in Switzerland without a legal adviser present."

The banker had clearly been given advance notice of the accounts which they wished to set up, and Dr Kraft passed over copies of the Trust's statutes and other formal documents appointing its directors, etc. Herr Lerner also asked to see the Minister's passport and called an assistant to take a copy for the files. He smiled at the Minister and produced a large folder clearly labelled 'Citizens of Kwandia Trust'. He tipped out a chequebook, a paying-in book and a plastic bank card from the folder. He smiled again. "Of course, most transactions these days can be made by card or over the internet, but you would probably be surprised just how many of our clients still prefer traditional banking methods."

The Minister smiled back at Herr Lerner. He did not wish to tell him that only about 11 percent of the Kwandian population had access to the internet and that even then it was notoriously unreliable.

"I believe you have brought the first deposit with you in person."

The Minister delved into his inside pocket and produced the two envelopes. After checking, he opened one of them and passed the money order from The Doorstep Foundation for ten million US Dollars. Herr Lerner smiled as he took the order from him and reached for his mobile phone. With a few quick taps, he announced that the amount would be 9.9 million Swiss Francs, which would be the currency of the account.

The Minister nodded." I believe you also deal in cryptocurrency?" The young banker smiled again. "Indeed, we do. Since last year, Zug has accepted digital currency, although all such receipts are immediately converted into Swiss Francs. We are gaining a reputation as 'Crypto Valley' because of the large number of companies engaged in cryptocurrency which are setting up here." He started to reel off names such as Etherium, Cardano, Polkadot and, of course, Bitcoin Suisse. It was now the Minister's turn to smile.

He then withdrew the second envelope from his pocket and produced a second money order made out to himself for the more modest sum of a hundred thousand US Dollars. The banker was pre-prepared and opened a second folder, this time in the name of Nouha Kyabou. They repeated the routine for the first bank account. However, before handing over the paperwork, he had a question for the Minister. "Swiss regulations require a personal account to be attached to a named individual, and we must, of course, assure ourselves of the identity and credentials of the account holder, which is why I asked to see your passport. However, it is not necessary for the paperwork connected with the account to be designated with your name if you do not wish it. Each account has its own unique number, which may be used on all documents, and we are not obliged to disclose the name of the account holder to third parties. Therefore, I have taken the liberty of preparing a numbered account for you, but if you wish your name to be on the chequebooks, etc., I can easily arrange it."

The Minister indicated his approval. He was more than happy with this arrangement. He turned to Dr Kraft, who immediately took the hint. "There is now just the small matter of the Minister's honorarium."

The Minister beamed at his attorney. 'Honorarium', he thought. What a splendid word. It must be Latin. There was nothing like Latin for giving some class to a transaction, which, in other words, might have sounded slightly shady, which would not do at all. He decided he liked Dr Kraft.

Herr Lerner also smiled. "Of course, I have prepared a monthly standing order between the two accounts for 10,000 Swiss Francs, which I believe was the amount mentioned."

The Minister and his lawyer left the bank and

returned to Dr. Kraft's office. Before he could leave, the minister had one more task to complete. The efficient lawyer had already prepared the necessary documentation, and after a cursory glance, the Minister pushed the documents into a white envelope supplied by the lawyer, sealed it down, and tucked it into his inside jacket pocket, which had previously held the money orders brought from Kwandia. "Thank you; that seems to be all."

The Minister was a happy man as he relaxed in the BMW on his way back to Zurich Airport. He also thought of himself as a clever man. The idea of setting up the Verein was brilliant. He could truly tell the Americans that the money from their charity had been placed in trust for the citizens of Kwandia. The fact that he was the sole signatory was, of course, for security reasons. He was perfectly entitled to charge up expenses such as a hotel stay in Paris and other 'incidentals' for his wife. Likewise, his 'honorarium' was not unreasonable for managing the trust. Such entities did not run themselves. And should he ever come under investigation, they would find only a modest amount in his own personal account with the Swiss bank compared with the substantial sum held on behalf of the Kwandian people. He privately congratulated himself on the cleverness of his scheme, and his smile grew even broader.

# Chapter 15 - The Gathering

The invitation to the memorial gathering for Owen Lewis had come by means of a telephone call from Mrs Lewis's sister, Ellen, earlier in the week, and Big Ben was chiming six o'clock in the evening as Rob and Declan sat in the back of a taxi making its way to a hotel in a side street somewhere between Victoria and Westminster. Rob was getting increasingly worried that time was passing, and they had made no real progress in understanding the purpose behind the vaccination programme in Kwandia. He was also very anxious to put Simon Fellowes in the picture, but he realised only too well the risks associated with doing so. The difficulties of getting a message to Simon made those risks even greater.

He told Declan of his conversation with Simon during his visit to England when he had spelled out the instructions for getting in touch with him. "The problem, Dec, is that internet availability and quality in Kwandia is limited to say the least. His email address is also that of his organisation, and we cannot regard it as secure. If the wrong people became aware of it, his life could well be in danger."

"And so might ours!" Declan agreed with Rob but was more sanguine than his friend about the speed of the vaccine programme in Kwandia. "Things move slowly in Africa, as I am sure you know only too well. If the aim is to cover the whole population, then we have a few weeks yet before things start to happen."

Rob was thoughtful. "I guess you are right. Let us hope we meet some people tonight who can shed some light on things."

The hotel entrance at which the taxi drew up was more impressive than they had expected, and Rob noted that it claimed to have four stars. As instructed, they made their way to the Frobisher Room and were further surprised not only by the size and opulence of the room but also the number of people already milling about with drinks in hand and chatting in small groups. There must have been at least a hundred or more in attendance.

Upon entering, they were met by a small reception party consisting of Mrs Lewis and her sister, accompanied by a small, round man. At a guess, they put him in his early thirties. He was prematurely bald with fleshy lips and bright blue eyes, and he had a notable twinkle suggesting impish humour behind his formal demeanour. Jerry Steinberg was not much taller than the two sisters beside him, and Rob had to bend quite low to shake his hand. "I'm delighted to meet you guys. Margaret has told me a lot about you." The voice was unmistakably American, and his presence in the welcoming committee suggested to Declan that he may well have financed the evening reception. He was intrigued to know where he fitted into the picture.

It was Margaret Lewis who enlightened him. "Jerry became a dear friend of my husband after he set up his practice in London and helped him often with the legal side of things. He had already become quite a celebrity in America after the Benson case, which was one of the biggest ever settlements by a pharmaceutical company. Jerry was the lead attorney; over twenty million dollars, wasn't it, Jerry?"

Declan imagined that his fee for such a case could certainly pay for any number of evening receptions and gave an admiring nod of approval. Jerry was quick to interject. "But it's not only about money. I am no great fan of Big Pharma and I became known for helping those who had the courage to expose their wrongdoings. My practice in the States continues to flourish without me, so I came to the UK for a new challenge and because there was no one here really specialising in this line of work at the time."

Rob was interested. "And have you found much work here?"

"More than I ever imagined," was the swift reply. It surprised Rob, and he frowned. "Well, good for your business, but I am not sure what it says about our medical profession."

Jerry did not want to go further down that path, particularly with a Harley Street doctor, and quickly turned the conversation to their current investigation and why they were there. "Your case is intriguing, if you don't mind me saying so, because I think there is more to it than meets the eye. I also think I can point you toward someone who can help you."

He turned to Mrs Lewis as more people started to enter the room. "Look, if we don't get a chance to talk more this evening, maybe you can come to my office in the morning." He produced his card, which Declan took before Rob could react and gave the attorney one of his own. But it was Rob who spoke. "I am afraid we were not planning to appoint a legal firm for this." Jerry caught on immediately. "I am not looking to sign you up as clients, and I can assure you that no fees will be involved. Besides, I am not sure I can assist you in any legal way, but I do have many contacts, and I believe one of them will be able to steer you in the right direction."

"We were hoping someone here tonight might be able to do that."

"So, they might, and I wish you luck, but my offer stands. Come to my office at 10 a.m. tomorrow if you can. After all, you have nothing to lose."

After detaching themselves from the welcoming party, the two men turned towards the mass of people in the room, who were mostly gathered in small groups, busy in conversation and enjoying the wine and canapes provided by a posse of serving staff. Rob had never felt comfortable on such occasions and hesitated before moving forward to join the throng. Declan, on the other hand, was in his element. Rob remembered that there was no one he knew who could 'work a room' like his friend. Give him two hours with a hundred people, and he could guarantee he would have met ninety-eight of them by closing time and probably learned their entire life histories. Rather than branch out alone, he decided to tag along with Declan.

He was also not surprised when the Irishman made straight for an attractive blonde woman of around thirty who was chatting with two older women. "Those glasses look nearly empty" Declan raised his hand to prevent a waiter from walking past and directed him to recharge the women's glasses. They smiled their thanks as Declan introduced himself and then turned to his more reserved companion. "This is Dr Robson Ford". Declan somehow made it sound more of an announcement than an introduction, as if he were deliberately trying to impress his audience and inflate the importance of his friend. Rob returned their smiles but felt the women looked more puzzled than impressed. Nevertheless, they had joined their conversation, and Declan was soon in full flow.
"So, what is your connection with Professor Lewis?"

It was the blonde who answered. "It is my mother, Carol, who has the real connection. He gave her help and advice when she was dismissed from her company for questioning the validity of some of the data they published from clinical trials that had been carried out concerning a new drug. She took up the issue with senior management in the company but was ignored. Then, worse still, she became the victim of a campaign to discredit her, accusing her of making errors in her work and breaching company regulations. In the end, she threatened to blow the whistle, so they sacked her on some trumped up charge." Her mother, who was standing beside her, nodded her agreement and spoke up. "I consulted a lawyer about fighting my case, and he introduced me to Professor Lewis. He was very supportive, but after much discussion, it was decided not to proceed. Frankly, I had had enough grief already and did not want to put myself through the stress of a court hearing."

Rob thought her case echoed Professor Lewis's own case. He had been a much more senior employee than this woman, but he began to wonder how many cases there were like hers, which never saw the light of day.

The third woman in the group introduced herself as a former editor of a professional medical journal but now retired. Rob saw her as a representative of the medical establishment and immediately shot her a question. "Are you not shocked by Carol's story?" He was disappointed by her reply. The woman shrugged her shoulders and gave him a rather condescending look. "Dr Ford, I regret to say that cases like those of Carol and Professor Lewis are only too common in the pharmaceutical and medical world. Very little shocks me anymore."

Rob was taken aback by the frankness of the reply. "But surely someone in your position would have been able to unmask such goings on."

The woman gave a thin smile. "If only! It is one thing to suspect or even know of such manipulation, but it is quite another to get the evidence to prove it. There are such things as libel laws in our country; believe me, these companies would not hesitate to use them. There is also a less edifying reason, I have to admit. We relied on the cooperation of many of these organisations for much of our published material, not to mention a large slice of our advertising revenue. My publishers would think very carefully before upsetting any of them, particularly the big boys."

Declan had been uncharacteristically quiet for the last few minutes but suddenly found his voice. "How far would these people go to cover their tracks?"

She hesitated before replying. Perhaps she had sensed what was coming next. If so, she was right.

"Do you believe Professor Lewis committed suicide?" Declan could not have put it more bluntly.

"Well, I have heard the rumours, and I rather guess that most of the people in this room don't believe that he did. All I can say is that even the suspicion of such a crime in this country was beyond my experience when I was working."

"In this country?" Declan picked up on those words.

"Well, there were always a few juicy stories coming out of America, even some involving their security forces. Those corporations are very powerful."

Rob was becoming increasingly disturbed by the conversation. "What about the regulatory bodies and the global health authorities? Would they not pick up errors or omissions in product trials?"

"I am sorry to say that over the years, I have seen those organisations fall more and more under the influence of the international corporations. I sometimes think they actually run them. But you should talk to Arthur over there. He used to work for one of them."

She waved her arm in the direction of a small, wiry man in his early sixties who came across to join them. But before they could interrogate Arthur Fisher, the crowded room was silenced by the sound of a large gong, and Jerry Steinberg was seen to be stepping up on a small, raised dais. He addressed the audience as 'Dear Friends' and went on to give a brief but sincere eulogy to Professor Owen Lewis, 'A great scientist and a great man'. He spoke for about eight minutes and stepped down to warm applause. Rob thought it was tastefully done and was glad he did not go on for too long and also that nobody else saw fit to follow him onto the rostrum. He hated those funerals where speaker after speaker felt it necessary to contribute long valedictions with reminiscences and anecdotes that meant something to the speaker but were often lost on the rest of the congregation.

When Jerry had stepped down, they turned back to introduce themselves to Arthur. "Which organisation did you work for?" asked Declan. His eyes lit up when the man replied that it was MAGIC. "So, you may have come across a character called Professor Rafal Glik."

"Glik!" The man's lips curled up in disgust, but he quickly straightened his face into a more neutral expression. After all, he could not be sure of the two men he had just met, one of whom had been introduced as a doctor. "Are you friends of his?"

Declan grinned "Not exactly, but we have come across his name in connection with a vaccine programme in Africa which we are currently investigating." Declan gave a quick description of the situation in Kwandia and their misgivings about the vaccine. He was careful not to give too much away, particularly their discovery about the vaccine's contents. "It seems Glik may have been influential in getting MAGIC to back this project, but he also seems to have connections with the company supplying it."

The man nodded his head. "That would not surprise me at all. I would not trust Glik further than I could throw him. In fact, he is one of the main reasons I quit that organisation." Declan and Rob were now all ears. They had drifted away from the three women so Arthur could say whatever he wanted to say in confidence. "I had been increasingly concerned by the way MAGIC operated and its close ties with big pharma. It was becoming more concerned with financial return than providing poorer countries with access to medicines. I went with Glik as part of a small delegation to an African country which I shall not name."

Declan wondered why he would not name the country but noted that he had glanced at Rob as he said it. Perhaps he was frightened of giving offence.

"The object of our visit was to seek cooperation in testing out a new anti-malaria drug. It had been through the usual preclinical trials but now needed to be tested on humans. This country was chosen because of its high incidence of malaria. There was no reason to suppose that it would be harmful to humans, but the local medical authorities were extremely wary, having had adverse experiences with pharmaceutical companies in the past. Glik explained that the clinical trials would be carried out by our organisation, not the companies themselves, and they would fully comply with internationally recognised protocols. However, the locals were still hesitant, and I sensed at the meeting that they were on the point of rejecting the proposal. It was at this point that the conversation turned sour, at least from my point of view."

"How so?" Declan was getting very interested now.

"The company which made this new drug also supplied a number of other products to the country, most notably a range of antibiotics for the treatment of various diseases. Glik reminded their chief medical officer of this fact and also pointed out that most of the products were sold to them at well below the market price at which they were sold to countries in Western Europe. I knew this was not true, but I could now see how the conversation was going."

Declan was ahead of him. "I know what you are going to tell me. They were told to participate in these trials or no more cheap medicines. Am I right?"

"Yes, exactly right, although Glik phrased it rather less bluntly. Of course, the Africans caved in because they had very little choice. I was so disgusted that I resigned from the organisation immediately when we returned from Africa." The friends murmured their admiration for the man's action, but Rob also wanted to know the outcome of the trials.

"Well, I had left MAGIC before the trials started, but I kept in touch with my colleagues. Sad to say, the programme was aborted after only two months due to the levels of adverse symptoms experienced by the participants. No deaths were reported, but I am ashamed to admit that had there been any, I believe they would have been covered up."

His reply rather shocked Rob. "I understand there

have been several major claims made against pharmaceutical companies in Africa, but I presume that no such claim was made in this case."

"You presume correctly, Dr Ford. They could not risk doing that and losing access to a whole range of medicines."

Declan turned to his friend. "Makes you wonder how many more cases there are like this which never see the light of day." Rob frowned but nodded in agreement with Declan.

# Chapter 16 - Distressing Tales

The two men made their way slowly through the room, and each person they met had a distressing tale to tell. At one stage, Declan remarked it was like attending a whistleblowers' convention, but Rob pointed out that it was a lot more than that. Many of the people had simply resigned their positions and were too scared to blow the whistle. Declan had to agree. "Not surprising when you consider the fate of some of those who did."

They had just been talking to the widow of an American doctor who had published doubts about a pharmaceutical product which was widely used in the United States. Not only that, but the Doctor who specialised in natural remedies had claimed that there was a far cheaper cure available. According to his widow, the latter claim seemed to provoke the sharpest reaction. First, his surgery was vandalised, but when that did not work, some of his remedies were discredited in the medical press, and he was even hauled before the medical board of the State in which he worked. There was some minor damage to his reputation, but his practice continued to thrive. Then, one day, he met with a fatal accident, a hit-and-run driver who was never caught. 'The police didn't try too hard to find them." The woman had contacted Jerry Steinberg's firm, but there was little point in pursuing a legal route without evidence. However, through Jerry, she had met others who had suffered adverse experiences at the hands of big pharma, including some whose partners' lives had been terminated in suspicious circumstances.

She had kept in touch with Jerry, who had told her of the Professor Lewis incident. There were echoes of her own case, so she decided to fly to London for a short holiday. She not only wanted to meet up with Jerry again but also offer any support she could to the Professor's family. She had long since lost faith in the American justice system but was shocked to hear of similar happenings in the UK. It was also how she had met ex-Chief Inspector Mike Robbins, whom she introduced to Rob and Declan.

The former policeman explained to them that he had taken early retirement from the force after being 'heavily leaned on' to soft-pedal an investigation into a serious assault. The victim had been a laboratory assistant at a pharmaceutical company who had rather naively written to the local paper complaining that he had been told to falsify test results where he worked. He had been sacked from his post but continued to repeat what the company described as 'unfounded and spurious allegations'. One day, he was found in the gutter near his home, very badly beaten up and lucky to survive. Mike Robbins said that his investigation had made rapid progress, but he was then called into his superior's office and told to slow things down. The instruction had come from the highest level, and there was a strong hint that the case would be shelved. It was clear to Mike that external pressure had been brought to bear, and he was pretty convinced where from. It was the last straw for him, so he negotiated his exit from the force.

As the evening progressed, the two men were experiencing very different emotions. Rob was becoming increasingly despondent. He was not naive enough to believe that occasional malpractices might occur in his profession, but what he had learnt tonight suggested an altogether greater scale than he had imagined. Every barrel has one or two rotten apples, but the implication from some of the stories suggested not only widespread corruption in the industry but also in the higher echelons of the establishment, both here and internationally. He wondered whether some of the claims were exaggerated or even fictitious, but a sudden twinge of pain at the back of his head reminded him of the attack on his doorstep. There was nothing fictitious about that, nor the demise of Professor Lewis, which he was now more certain than ever was no suicide.

In contrast to the gloomy disposition of his friend, Declan was becoming more and more animated. For him, the gathering had turned into a marvellous networking opportunity, and his business cards were flying from his wallet, and his small notepad was rapidly filling up with phone numbers and email addresses. But then, spotting someone at the far end of the room, he hit the pause button.

Turning to Rob, he nudged his friend and nodded in the direction of the person he had seen. "That is

Colin Redfearn." The name meant nothing to Rob until Declan explained that he was the technical boffin who had carried out the tests on the vaccine at the laboratory near Cambridge. Rob considered the information before he spoke. "So, he is still working for Lewis's old company."

The man was in conversation with two other men who appeared from a distance to be almost interrogating him rather than just chatting. Declan started to make his way across the room, followed by Rob. When they saw them approach, the men talking to Redfearn turned abruptly towards the door and vanished from the room.

Declan was all smiles. "Good evening, Mr Redfearn."

"Well, it is Professor Redfearn, actually, Mr Walsh."

Redfearn looked slightly nervous, but Declan's smile only got broader. "Yes, of course, I must apologise, but allow me to introduce Dr Ford, who has been treating the patient injected with the vaccine you so kindly analysed for us. I'm sorry if we have frightened off your two friends."

Redfearn looked at Rob and then turned back to Declan. "They weren't friends, as it happens. In fact, I have never met them before, although I am surprised they rushed off when you arrived because it was you and your mysterious vaccine they were asking me about."

It was now the turn of the two friends to look nervous. Declan tried to sound casual. "Oh really, and what were you able to tell them?"

"Not very much, really. I was about to explain the rather curious results of our analysis when you arrived."

Declan persisted. "Did you catch their names, where they were from, or why they were asking?"

Although Declan delivered his questions with a reassuring smile, Rob sensed that Professor Redfearn felt slightly irritated at what appeared to him to be another cross-examination. Furthermore, his answer did nothing to ease their concerns. "Come to think of it, they did not introduce themselves but launched straight into their questions, a bit like you, if I may say so."

Declan was quick with his retort. "Sorry again, Professor, but of course, in our case, you do know who we are."

That comment was met with a quizzical look from Redfearn. "Well, actually, I know very little about you, Mr Walsh, other than you were obviously both good friends of Owen. I also have no knowledge about the origins of that so-called vaccine you brought me to analyse. Owen gave me no background information and wanted the whole transaction to remain confidential. However, it appears that others are also interested in its contents. Perhaps you could enlighten me as to why."

Redfearn had neatly turned the interrogation round so that it was Declan who had to come up with an explanation. "I'm afraid we were as surprised by the vaccine's contents as you, Professor Redfearn, and equally puzzled as to who else might be interested. All I can tell you is that Owen was right to stress that the matter should remain confidential."

He and Rob felt they had exhausted the usefulness of Colin Redfearn and took their leave of him by catching Jerry Steinberg's eye on the other side of the room. He was still talking to Margaret Lewis, but they had now moved away from the entrance and were nearer the back of the room. It was getting late, and many of the guests had already left. The two friends had decided to follow suit, but before doing so, there was one more piece of information they would hope to obtain. It was Rob who took up the matter with Mrs Lewis. "Do you happen to have a guest list for tonight?"

The question surprised her a little, and her answer disappointed Rob. "I am afraid not. It was never intended to be a formal occasion. There were some specific invitees, such as yourselves, for example, but otherwise, anyone who knew my husband was welcome as if it were a conventional wake, I suppose. Word soon got around, judging by the number of people here."

"Yes indeed." Rob smiled. "It was a very pleasant

evening. Thank you for inviting us."

Jerry, however, was more curious. "Were you looking for someone in particular?"

Declan stepped in and tried to sound nonchalant. "Not really, but there were a couple of types talking to Colin Redfearn, who didn't seem to want to talk to us."

Jerry shrugged his shoulders. "Maybe they were current employees of Owen's old firm who had come to pay their respects but didn't really want to be seen here. Otherwise, did you meet any interesting folk who might be able to shed some light on your investigation?"

It was now Declan's turn to shrug his shoulders. "We met lots of interesting people, but regrettably, no one who could solve our mystery."

Jerry nodded sagely. "I am not really surprised. Having heard your story, I believe that the answer lies outside the strictly medical sphere. I think there are other factors at play here, and I know just the person who may be able to help. I will contact her later when I get back."

"Later?" Declan raised his eyebrows. "I hope she will appreciate being woken up in the middle of the night."

Jerry laughed. "Well, this person is on the East

Coast, and don't forget the USA is five hours behind us. It will be early evening there. "

Both Declan and Rob had been seriously perturbed by the two men who were talking to Redfearn, and neither of them 'bought' the explanation offered by Jerry. Something in his tone also suggested he was not convinced by it either. Perhaps he did not want to display his true suspicions in front of Mrs Lewis. He would not want to upset her or add to her grief. They were, therefore, pleased when he repeated his earlier invitation.

"Can I expect to see you gentlemen at my office tomorrow morning?"

Rob and Declan looked at each other and nodded in unison "We'll be there."

# Chapter 17 - Jerry Steinberg

It was very late when Rob finally got home, and Alice had long since gone to bed. She appeared to be fast asleep as he slipped silently under the sheets, trying hard not to wake her. He felt exhausted, not so much physically, but the evening had taken its toll on his mental state. He lay back and closed his eyes, hoping that sleep would come and rid him of the turmoil in his mind. Three things troubled him. Firstly, the two men they saw talking to Redfearn. Who were they, and what did they want? Their presence at the hotel meant that he and Declan were still being shadowed, and the thought worried him.

Secondly, he was beginning to question his own motivation in continuing with their investigation. If it was not primarily medical, as Jerry had hinted at, why should he become involved? He also felt that his very status in life was somehow called into question. He had come a long way, from a boy in a small African village to a respected member of the establishment, a Harley Street doctor and married into a family on the fringes of British aristocracy. The further they progressed with the investigation, the more he began to question the true values which supported his comfortable lifestyle. It was an unpleasant thought, but he persuaded himself that he owed the people of Kwandia to continue his quest. Lives might depend upon it. This line of thinking led him to the third of his worries.

He was becoming increasingly frustrated with their lack of progress. He and Declan had learnt a lot this evening, but none of the acquired knowledge brought them any closer to understanding what was actually happening in Kwandia and the underlying purpose of the vaccination programme. He fell asleep, hoping that tomorrow's meeting with Jerry Steinberg would unlock at least some of the mystery. Time was running out.

***********************************

At the appointed hour, the two friends arrived outside the offices of Steinberg and Paul in Chancery Lane. They were one of many law firms housed in this street, and the building, though old, had little architectural merit. However, the reception area inside was bright, modern and attractive. Declan awarded a similar description to Laura, who welcomed them with a friendly smile from behind the polished wooden counter where she sat.

Having taken their names and provided them with their visitor badges, she led them through the glass security gate into a short hallway. She took their orders for coffee. The choice offered rivalled that of Starbucks. There were more smiles as she explained that Jerry's conference call was overrunning, but he had asked her to show them directly into his office. "He sends his apologies, but I am sure he will not be long." Declan thought he caught the trace of an American accent in Laura's voice but couldn't be sure. Maybe she was English, but you can pick up accent and vocabulary if you work with Americans all day.

Jerry's office was large and almost exactly square. The predominant feature was a large pedestal desk in expensive-looking polished wood with a green leather inlaid surface. Behind the desk was a large swivel chair in matching green leather. They sat themselves down in the two visitor chairs in front of the desk, which were also upholstered in green leather but more upright and functional than Jerry's large 'executive' chair.

Looking around the room, Rob was struck by the fact that all four walls were completely lined with glass-fronted wooden bookcases and every shelf was packed solid with legal tomes of similar size but varying content. They were a mixture of American and UK origin and, to the untrained eye, did not appear to be classified in any particular order. Although Rob suspected that such was the number of books, there must be some method to their arrangement. One section caught his eye in which all the books had the words case law or legal precedents in the title. This jogged his memory of an earlier conversation with Declan, and he laughed out loud at the thought that entered his head.

Declan gave his friend a quizzical look. "What's so funny?" Rob's answer was just one word, "Exhibit One!"

Declan caught on immediately and also laughed. "Yes. Neurotechnology and the Law. Just think if Jerry was injected with a microchip, he could get rid of all the books in this room."

Rob laughed again. "He'd have to paper the walls without all those bookcases."

Declan was pleased to see his friend so amused. He had noticed how sombre he had become in recent weeks and was grateful for anything which could lighten his mood.

At that moment, the door opened, and Jerry Steinberg bounced in, full of apologies as he shook both of their hands. They watched silently as he walked round the desk, but instead of taking his chair, he went to the bookcase behind it and slid open one of the glass doors. From there, he removed two of the largest volumes and placed them on his chair. Then, bending down, he opened a cupboard in the bottom right-hand side of his desk and took out a large square cushion covered in matching green leather. Placing the cushion on top of the books, he climbed up and took his seat, peering down on his guests like a medieval monarch on his throne.

"Let me show you guys something." He opened a drawer in his desk and withdrew two folders. From one of them, he took out a bunch of closely typed A4 sheets of paper stapled together and waved them in front of the two men but did not pass them over. "These are lists of claims made against pharmaceutical companies in the last decade. There are pages and pages of them."

Rob raised his eyebrows in astonishment at the sheer volume of cases. Declan was less surprised. Jerry Steinberg explained further.

"They cover a wide range of transgressions from unethical experimentation through to wrongful dismissal of whistle-blowers, but by far the largest category by number is what are known as 'off-label' marketing of drugs. You are probably familiar with the practice where an approved drug for one medical condition is sold to treat another without undergoing the normal regulatory testing required. As a medical practitioner, Dr Ford, you may have faced such circumstances occasionally?"

Rob nodded in agreement but explained to the lawyer that whilst he may prescribe a medicine not yet on the approved list in the UK, he would always ensure it was backed up by scientific research and usually had also been approved in another reliable jurisdiction.
"All medicines carry risks whether approved or not, and one has to make judgements, particularly in serious conditions when all else has failed."

Jerry gave him a benign smile from his throne. "Of course, but regrettably, not every drug company is as scrupulous as you. In fact, some of the largest monetary settlements have been for off-label marketing." He then returned the papers to the folder and picked up the other one. This contained only one sheet of paper. "You may find this of interest. Before you arrived, I asked my receptionist Laura to run a search program through that claims list to find any mention of Professor Rafal Glik."

Again, he waved the sheet of paper at them without passing it over. However, they could see that it contained a list of about twenty or so cases. "You can see that he has been quite a busy boy, judging by how many times his name crops up."

Jerry sat back in his chair. "Whilst these papers are interesting, I do not think they will provide you with the answers you are looking for. As I told you last night, I believe the pharmaceutical and medical angle is no more than a cover for some ulterior motive, but I am afraid I can only speculate on what that might be. You may remember I also told you I had a contact back home who might be able to help. I spoke to her last night, but she needs a lot more information from you. However, she did throw out one suggestion."

The friends were all ears.

"Have either of you heard of 'Aadhaar'?"

They looked blank. Declan grinned, "Sounds like an animal."

Another benign smile from Jerry. "It is a project

which has been developed in India since 2009 and has been described by the World Bank as 'The most sophisticated ID programme in the world'. Over 1.3 million people have been issued an Aadhaar card containing basic demographic and biometric information such as a photograph, ten fingerprints and two iris scans. These are all stored in a centralised database. Jim Doors is a great fan of this project and believes all countries should follow India's lead."

Rob was thoughtful. "But surely many countries already have ID cards, particularly in Europe. What's so special about the Indian version?"

"Well, in most countries, using ID cards is for security and convenience. An all-purpose ID card is useful whenever you need to prove that you are who you are. But Aadhaar has gradually developed much further. In theory, they are not compulsory, but they have become mandatory by indirect means. Many private and public benefits have become linked to Aadhaar ID numbers, such as food aid, cooking gas subsidies, sim cards for mobile phones, banking facilities, etc. It can be used to store all personal information, including medical history, religious affiliation, and financial details. The list is endless."

This was all very interesting, but Rob wondered what it had to do with Kwandia. Declan was beginning to see, and Jerry confirmed his suspicion. "One major problem with Aadhaar is that it is a card-based system, and cards can be lost, stolen or compromised. Suppose someone invented a means by which the same information could be loaded onto a microchip and injected into a person. Using blockchain technology, every man, woman and child in a population could be linked to a central database. The possibilities are mind-blowing, and the software would be worth a fortune."

Declan was now getting excited. "So, you think that the Kwandian project is a massive trial of such a system?"

"Well, it was an idea put to me by Velma, and it makes sense."

"Velma?"

"She was the lady I contacted last night. Her name is Velma Stanway, and she has become well-known in the States. At one time, she was a senior official in a central government department and then an investment banker in a major firm in Wall Street. She is now a freelance investment consultant and, more importantly, a very free thinker. Her willingness to use her background knowledge to expose dubious motives and corruption at the very highest level has made her many enemies among the financial elite. She is quite an expert on Jim Doors and the like."

Rob was pensive. "I can see the attraction of such a system, but why the need to conceal it behind a medical facade and to go to great lengths to prevent anyone from finding out about the vaccine?"

"My guess is that the local population would have been less keen to line up for an injection unless they felt there was a health benefit, but you are right, Doctor. There are many questions still unanswered, and Velma is certainly of the opinion that there is more to this affair than meets the eye. She also threw cryptocurrency into the conversation, but I did not really understand how that could fit in. However, she needs to have a lot more detail about the people involved and about the political situation in Kwandia. She would be interested in talking to you, and with her background knowledge of Jim Doors and the Doorstep Foundation, I am confident she can work it out for you."

"So, we need to contact this lady." Declan was eager to make progress.

Jerry gave him one of his smiles. "I'm afraid that will take some effort on your part."

The two men looked quizzical as Jerry continued. "Electronic communication with her is impossible except for a strict few who have access to her heavily encrypted network. I am one of those, but I cannot allow third parties to access it. The only way she will talk to you is face to face."

It was now Declan's turn to smile. "You mean we shall need to go to America? Where does she live exactly?"

"She lives and works in Connecticut, but she will not see you there, bearing in mind the risks involved with this project. She will stay with a friend in Naples, Florida, and you can meet there. So, guys, how do you fancy a long weekend in the sunshine?"

Jerry took their silence as acquiescence to his proposal, and before they could answer, he began issuing them more detailed instructions. "There are obviously people keeping an eye on you even if you are not being tailed night and day. I suggest, therefore, that you do not fly directly from Heathrow but go to Copenhagen and pick up a flight to Miami from there. In any case, you may well find it cheaper as you will not have to pay your country's extortionate departure tax. I also advise you to dress as tourists. Don't make it look like a business trip."

As they left his office, Rob reflected that behind Jerry's genial personality, there was a steely resolve and an inclination to call the shots. He seemed to have left them no choice but to follow his directions. How was he going to explain this to Alice? He glanced at Declan, who was grinning from ear to ear. He had no such concerns.

\*\*\*\*\*\*\*\*\*\*\*\*\*\*\*\*\*\*\*\*\*\*\*\*\*\*\*\*\*\*\*\*\*\*\*\*\*\*

Her first reaction surprised Rob. She burst out laughing. Then he realised it was because she thought he was joking. However, when she understood he was serious, her smile quickly vanished and was replaced by a worried frown. "Why on earth do you need to go to America just to see this person? What is so special about her?"

Rob repeated the explanation given to them by Jerry, adding, 'She is some sort of expert on Jim Doors.'

It did not convince Alice. "Let me remind you that the last expert you consulted ended up dead in a river in Sussex, and you have already had a bang on the head for your trouble. I don't want to have to come and fish you out of a Florida swamp."

Rob's attempt to reassure her by reminding her of Declan's presence seemed only to heighten her anxiety. Whilst she was very fond of the genial Irishman, she knew he was more of a risk taker than a risk avoider. "That is what frightens me most of all."

He quickly changed the subject. "What do you know about cryptocurrency? Is your firm a big investor?" Alice shook her head. "We don't invest in it, and we are not allowed to recommend it to our clients. Rob was intrigued. "Why not?" The reply was short and to the point. "Because it is an unregulated product."

"Oh, I see" Rob tried to sound as if he understood the significance of Alice's explanation, but she had a further question. "So, what has cryptocurrency got to do with your investigation?"

He shrugged his shoulders. "I haven't the faintest idea."

# Chapter 18 - Florida

Rob was not comfortable. He was distinctly uncomfortable. On the few recent occasions he had been on long-haul flights, it was always business class or even first class, but now he found himself cramped into a window seat in the economy section of an Airbus 350 from Copenhagen to Miami and was not looking forward to the next ten hours. Declan's expense allowance had restricted their options, so Rob's long legs were folded so his knees almost touched his chin.

Alice chose his 'casual tourist' attire, which consisted of a crisp white short-sleeved shirt and lightweight pale grey flannel trousers. Declan, of course, had opted for the full Hawaiian. A bright blue shirt covered in a coconut palm tree pattern. He wore beige jeans, which Rob guessed were some upmarket designer brand. They occupied two seats in a bank of three, the aisle seat being occupied by a shortish, thick-set man with a ruddy face and light sandy-coloured hair. When he spoke, Rob decided that his accent and his apparent outgoing personality marked him down as American. He felt sure the man would be regaling them with his life story at the earliest opportunity, so he closed his eyes and feigned sleep. Declan would know how to deal with him.

As it happened, Rob was only partially correct. The man was actually Swedish, although he had lived in America for sixteen years and built up a thriving interior design business. Rob assumed that this accounted for his American accent and possibly also for his genial disposition. He had not encountered many Swedish people in his life, but he once attended a medical seminar in Stockholm and remembered the local population as being mostly tall, often blond and very reserved in character, almost to the point of being taciturn. Tommy Ahlgren, as he had introduced himself, did not seem to fit this mould, and when he started asking questions about their visit, Rob began to get worried about who he might actually be.

"You guys looking forward to enjoying the delights of Miami?"

Declan smiled at the man. "Afraid we won't have much time in Miami as we are going straight on to Naples." Even as he spoke, he regretted giving the man this information and, like Rob, began to worry whether Tommy Ahlgren was quite as innocent as he seemed. He was also surprised by the Swede's reaction. A snort of laughter was not what he had expected. "You know what they say about Naples?" Declan shook his head but was sure that Tommy was about to tell him. "They say that Florida is the state where the old folks go, and Naples is where they go to visit their parents!" He laughed loudly at his own joke whilst Declan smiled politely.

But the man wasn't finished. "So many old folks are probably why it has so many golf courses. Thinks of itself as the world's golf capital and probably has more courses per head of population than any other resort in America." He glanced across at the sleeping Rob. "Your friend looks as though he can hit a mean golf ball." Declan nodded even though, so far as he knew, Rob had never been near a golf course in his life. More laughter came from the Swede. "Don't forget the number one local rule on every course. You get a free drop if your ball lands by a gator."

Declan laughed politely but decided to join his friend in trying to get some sleep. He closed his eyes and thought of his youth in Ireland when he did, in fact, play a lot of golf on the many courses available on the Emerald Isle. He remembered hazards such as bunkers and water, but thankfully, there were no alligators.

When they finally landed in Miami, the two men hung back slightly so that Tommy could get well ahead of them before going through passport control. They found the Hertz bus to take them to the car rental depot outside the airport. Rob was happy to let Declan do the driving whilst he appointed himself as navigator, even though the car had a built-in satnav. He had already done some research and discovered there were two route possibilities to drive to Naples. Both took about two hours, although the Interstate 75 Highway, which was a toll road known locally as Alligator Alley, was marginally quicker. The alternative was US Highway 41, which was called the Tamiami Trail.

It was reputedly less busy than the Interstate, and Rob thought this might be the better option since it would give them a greater chance of spotting any vehicle which might be following.

Highway 41 threaded its way through the outer suburbs of Miami but then turned into an almost deserted road with dense vegetation on either side, forming part of the vast swampy area known as the Everglades. They passed a few businesses offering boat tours and the occasional small settlement having a motor service station or a diner. Rob noticed that at least half of such places had the word 'gator' in their name. The almost complete absence of traffic or people made him wonder whether he had chosen the wisest route. After all, they were sitting ducks for anyone who wished to waylay them.

He was quietly mulling over his decision and nearly falling asleep when Declan suddenly slammed his foot on the brakes and pulled the car onto the wide grass verge beside the road. He opened the door, and before the dozing Rob could react, he sprinted back in the direction they had come, his bright blue shirt flapping in the Florida sunshine. He stopped after about one hundred yards and pointed his mobile phone at something away from the road. Beyond the grass verge, there was a ditch with running water and, beyond that, a steep grassy bank before the trees and vegetation in the distance.

As Rob caught him up, he saw what had caught

Declan's eye. Lazing on top of the bank were two magnificent specimens of the local reptile population. They appeared asleep, although Rob saw one eye open as Declan arrived. "What on earth are you doing?"

Declan clicked the camera on his phone a couple of times before turning to his friend. Well, we are supposed to be tourists, so I thought I might as well act like one." Rob was not impressed. "Well, we don't want to end up as dead tourists. You realise that those things can move fast when they want to, and they can swim!" The last few words were added when Declan tried to point out that there was a good distance between them as well as the ditch ."My dear friend, I am willing to bet those boys are  well used to human beings, probably posing for tourists all the time!" adding as an afterthought, "Actually, I thought you might like to go and join them so I could take a really good picture for Alice and the girls!"

"You mean, one last picture of your father before he was eaten by a crocodile!" Rob put his hand on Declan's shoulder and pushed him back towards the direction of the car whilst at the same time keeping a wary eye on the two creatures in case they showed any sign of movement. Declan laughed as he led the way back to the car. "Robbie, my boy, you have no sense of adventure."

They had booked a hotel that sat alongside the Naples marina and looked out onto a large expanse of water called Naples Bay. They had reserved what the Americans call an 'efficiency' room, which in this case consisted of two large beds with a small kitchenette area equipped with a microwave oven, an electric hob and a refrigerator. The small dining table and two chairs were ideal for making breakfast or a light meal.

By now, the men were getting hungry and decided to find the restaurant at the far end of the building, which had a fine view across the bay. Rob had obtained a road map of the area and discovered that Flamingo Drive, which was Velma's address, was on the opposite side of the bay towards the mouth of the Gordon River. As they walked in front of the hotel, he pointed out to Declan where he thought they would be aiming for the following morning. There were inlets at regular intervals on that side of the bay with parallel running streets so that all of the properties in the streets would have gardens leading down to the water. Even from a distance, they could guess that Villa Rosa was likely to be a luxurious property in an impressive location.

# Chapter 19 - Velma

The men felt refreshed after a good night's sleep and an American breakfast in the hotel's breakfast bar, where the non-stop banter between some of the residents and the staff provided early morning entertainment.

They found Villa Rosa with no difficulty. As the name implied it was a substantial pinkwashed house set well back from the road with a large driveway in front of it. Declan steered the car around a well-established oleander tree and parked alongside a detached garage, which he estimated would take at least three cars. They had obviously been observed as the front door opened just before they reached it. The woman who greeted them was tall, grey-haired and wore a long flowing Kaftan-style robe which nearly reached her ankles. Rob judged that such a garment would be ideal in the heat of the 'Sunshine State'. "Velma Stanway?" It was Declan who enquired. "No, I am Dorothy Parnell, and this is my house. Velma is my houseguest for the week, but she is expecting you. Please come in."

They entered a spacious hallway, and through a back window, they caught a glimpse of the yachts sailing on Naples Bay. The villa was not only opulent but also perfectly sited for magnificent views. They were shown into an equally large living room with light oak flooring and expensive-looking Persian rugs. Towards the picture window at the rear was a long settee, and perched on a small pile of silk-covered cushions was a tiny woman sitting with her legs crossed and drawn up so that her feet were on the settee. It immediately reminded Rob of Jerry Steinberg's unconventional throne-like seating in London, and the thought flashed through his mind that perhaps they were related, although he could see no family resemblance. Her face was well-tanned, and her sitting position meant that the pale blue Bermuda shorts rode up to reveal knees and shins, which were nut brown in colour, suggesting that she spent more than just the odd week with her friend in Florida.

She made no attempt to get up but smiled a greeting and motioned them towards the two chairs in front of her. Rob began by apologising for causing her to temporarily relocate to Florida from her base in Connecticut and tried to reassure her that it was not their intention to put her at risk in any way. She laughed. "Gentlemen, I flatter myself that although I am an occasional thorn in the flesh of the establishment here, I am sufficiently well known in this country to be a very unlikely candidate for elimination without a major public outcry. No, guys, we are down here for your safety, not mine." Declan took up the conversation. "I am pretty sure we were not followed, so I am equally sure that no one actually knows we are here."

Velma nodded. "That is good to hear, Mr Walsh."

"Call me Declan, please and my colleague Doctor

Ford is known as Rob."

"As it happens, I was due a visit to stay with Dottie, who is one of my oldest and dearest friends. We go back to our days in Wall Street when she was one of the sharpest cookies in the investment bank for which we both worked then. She may be Dottie by name, but she is certainly not dotty by nature." She smiled at her rather feeble joke.

The men then noticed that the other woman had left the room but returned at that moment carrying a tray with four glasses of iced tea, a favourite beverage of Americans but not really to Declan's taste, although Rob found it quite refreshing. Dorothy, or Dottie, as she was known, pulled up a chair to listen to the conversation. Velma quickly got down to business. "Jerry in London has given me an outline of the events in your story, but I need a lot more detail to be sure of my ground before I offer any opinion. So, Doctor Rob, I am sorry, but I will have to ask you to go through the whole saga from the beginning. As much detail as possible please. Leave out nothing."

Rob cast his mind back to the day young Julian Fellowes came into his surgery exhibiting all the symptoms of tuberculosis. He explained his unease at learning of the vaccine he had received in Kwandia and went on to describe the efforts he had made to find out more about it. Velma listened intently to his story, but from time to time, she jotted something down in a small notebook which she had produced from a handbag at her side. Rob observed that she made notes when he mentioned the names of the companies he had contacted.

Declan took up the story. He described the bugging of Rob's surgery and his family home, which caused Velma to raise her eyebrows, but she said nothing. He then recounted their meeting with Professor Lewis, whose name Velma seemed to recognise. She frowned and looked at her friend when Declan mentioned the killing of their dog, Buster. He observed the exchange of looks and thought he heard the word 'CIA', muttered under her breath. "I am afraid there is worse to come." Velma nodded and made her first brief comment. "I know."

"Shortly after our visit to the professor, my good friend here was attacked on his own doorstep and received a nasty bang on the head as well as a good kicking." Velma made another note. Rob thought he should mention the two conversations with his father-in-law and Simon Fellowes.
"It appears that in Kwandia, the vaccine project is being driven by the finance minister, Nouha Kyabou, who is apparently very ambitious and seen by some as having his eyes on the presidency."

Velma made another note and commented that it was a detail of which she was not aware.
Rob continued. "We obtained samples of the vaccine from my young patient's father when he came back to England on leave from his NGO, which is running a major water project. He complained

that the vaccine project had diverted resources from his own but reinforced the view that there was rivalry between President Diaby and his finance minister. He was also annoyed by another potential diversion of resources, which was the discovery of lithium ore in the west of the country. He thought that this was the reason the president had received a delegation from China recently."

Velma made another note and also another comment. "Lithium, you say. That is very rare in Africa. Most lithium in the world is found either in South America or the USA, Australia and China."

Declan then related his efforts to get the vaccine samples analysed and how Professor Lewis had used a contact at his old firm to get the analysis done at one of their outlying laboratories. They were astonished to find it contained nothing more than a weak saline solution and then, a few days later, even more astonished to discover it concealed one of the smallest microchips known to man. He described the information about various microchip projects which he had obtained from Mackenzie's company. A later conversation with young Julian Fellowes revealed that the local inhabitants were all injected in the hand between the thumb and forefinger, which struck them as curious. "That is fascinating." Velma gave a knowing smile.

At this point, Rob felt he should continue the narrative. "I regret to say tragedy then struck." He went on to describe the untimely demise of

Professor Lewis and the strange circumstances surrounding the discovery of his body. "Bizarre," commented Velma when he explained the link with the suicide of Virginia Woolf back in 1941. She spoke again. "And you don't think it was suicide?" Rob confirmed that he was pretty sure it was not. He had never exhibited any suicidal tendencies and had no reason for killing himself. He was happily married but left no note. What really troubled me was the actions of the police, who started off with a mindset of potential foul play but then suddenly changed their tune and could hardly wait to close the file for the whole episode.

"At a memorial event for Professor Lewis, we learnt a lot about corruption in the pharmaceutical industry, and we met Jerry Steinberg, who in turn referred us to you." The men sat back in their chairs, feeling they had now reached the end of their story.

By contrast, Velma sat up straighter. She handed her empty glass to her friend and suggested a further round of iced teas. Rob accepted, but Declan declined gracefully. As Dottie went off to fetch them, Velma started to outline her hypothesis. "This has all the hallmarks of a takeover." Rob wasn't sure what she meant. "A takeover?"

Velma gave a rueful smile. "I first have to explain something about my country. The USA is an empire builder. Historically, empires have been built by physical invasion followed by the seizure of valuable assets and subjugation of the indigenous population. Such actions would not be tenable in today's world, at least not in a country that holds itself out as a champion of freedom and democracy. So, it has to build its empire by gaining economic influence or even control. Henry Kissinger is reputed to have once voiced the opinion that 'America does not have friends or enemies, only interests.' What we have here seems like a small expansion of those interests."

Declan was on full alert. "You mean this affair is being orchestrated by the American government?"

Velma shook her head. "Not exactly. There is something else you need to know about America. Its government agencies, including security agencies such as the CIA, don't work only for the government."

Declan expressed surprise. "What do you mean?"

"Well, there are a group of people I call 'The Bills'."

"Who are the Bills?" Declan was intrigued.

"It is my term for the billionaires. Consider this. There are ten corporations, mostly American, which account for twenty-five percent of the value of the world's stock markets. There are probably no more than a dozen men, again mostly American, who own half of the world's wealth. These people are worth more individually than the entire economies of most countries in the world, particularly third-world countries like Kwandia. It would be naive to suppose that they do not exert a major influence on our government. Indeed, since most of our politicians owe their careers to their backing, some people believe they actually determine our policies and that the government is largely irrelevant."

Declan was quick to comment. "Do you think American voters appreciate this?"

Velma gave him one of her rueful smiles. "Possibly some do, but equally, they may not care. You have to understand that American culture is dominated by money. It is their religion and the only way they measure success." The men looked at each other, but it was Declan who spoke, "Surely an exaggeration?" The woman was unmoved. "You may say so, but look at the evidence. For example, we have just elected a new President who constantly boasted of his wealth and business success. Can you name any other country in the world where individual wealth would be seen as an electoral asset and vote winner? Most political leaders look to hide their wealth from the populace, even the unelected despots in totalitarian states."

Declan got the message but dived in with another question. "Why is Jim Doors buying up so much agricultural land in America?" Another wry smile from Velma. "That is another story and depends on how long you've got. But here's another statistic for you. Seventy per cent of the world's farmlands are now owned by one per cent of the world's farms. What better way to control the world's food supply than deciding what we eat and how the land is used? Cynics might say that climate change has something to do with it. By adding land to their portfolio of investments, The Doorstep Foundation can appear to become 'carbon neutral', and that great philanthropist Jim Doors can show how he is helping to save the planet."

At that point, the conversation paused as Dottie returned with the iced teas.

# Chapter 20 - Explanation

Suitably refreshed, Velma resumed her explanation. "I am pretty sure there is more than one strand to this affair, but let's start with the vaccine project. I was intrigued by the list of research projects you found currently being carried out to develop ultra-small microchips. It chimes with information I learned from a colleague a short while back. She had been to a tech exhibition in Copenhagen and met a Danish software company working on a joint enterprise with the US Navy developing an injectible microchip which could interact with one of the cryptocurrencies."

Rob remembered the conversation with Jerry Steinberg. "Do you think that is what is happening here?"

"It is a distinct possibility. You need to understand that Crypto is not so much a currency but a way of controlling a population. Every Central Bank in the world is racing to develop its own digital currency. China is believed to be the most advanced country, which is not really a surprise since it is a country that already exercises significant control over its people. However, projects like these need test beds and small third-world countries like Kwandia would be ideal. All of this software would operate on a platform owned and managed by one of the giant American tech corporations. So, what better way to control a country than to control its currency."

Rob was puzzled. "I understand what you are saying, but why should Jim Doors be involved in such a project? What's in it for him or his foundation?"

"Good thinking, Dr Rob. I guess that he has an interest in the software company behind it, but it is a long-term play, and your question is valid. He will also be looking for a more immediate return. As I said earlier, I am sure there is more than one strand to this business, and I am pretty sure I can see what the other interest might be. You mentioned the discovery of lithium ore. That would be a big prize and worth involving government agencies to protect."

This point particularly interested Rob, who could still feel the occasional twinge from the beating on his doorstep. "Are you saying that the CIA were responsible for my attack and Professor Lewis's demise?"

"Well, it is quite common for the CIA to carry out missions on foreign territories, but in the case of the UK, any local action could well have been subcontracted to MI6. They would also have better access to local police, which would explain the latter's reluctance to pursue the Professor Lewis case. Our security services often cooperate and work closely together, but you Brits don't take kindly to foreign powers operating on your own patch even if it is a friendly nation."

Her use of the term 'you Brits' caused the two men

to exchange a quick glance. One of them was born in Africa and the other in Ireland, although in Rob's case, he had obtained UK citizenship and held dual nationality, so he was unlikely to take offence. He hoped his Irish friend would not try to make a point with Velma. There were bigger issues at stake here. He was grateful when Declan let it pass. He could also see that Velma had reached a stage in her discourse when she was about to explain all.

"There were three important clues in your story which I noted down." She referred to her little notebook. "Firstly, the company making the vaccine is ME Chemicals. Secondly, the President has recently received a delegation from China; thirdly, the President has a rival waiting in the wings to take over should anything untoward happen to him. I believe I can put together a viable scenario as to what is going on here." The men were all ears.

"You could not trace the ownership of MF Chemicals, but I can hazard a pretty good guess. Jim Doors owns a company called ME Corporation, which is also registered in Delaware. My bet is that ME Chemicals is a subsidiary of that. I also happen to know that the 'ME' in ME Corporation originally stood for 'Metal Extraction', and it operates a rare metals refinery in Africa, Mauritania, I believe, but don't hold me to that." Declan was nodding his head. "Makes sense!"

"My next guess is that President Diaby was approached by the Americans about the lithium deposits, but he kept them at arm's length. He intended to play all ends against the middle, so he invited the Chinese along. However, the Americans did not want to enter a bidding war and looked for another way in. They found it in the form of the Minister of Finance. It would not be the first time the Americans have helped to overthrow a government, and keeping the Chinese out will resonate politically back home. I suspect that some money has changed hands, and in return for their backing, the Minister will have promised to grant them mineral rights in the country. The 'vaccine' project acts not only as a brilliant camouflage for their real purpose but if I am right about the currency aspect, it offers them another major lever of control over the country."

Declan was now becoming animated. "It all fits, doesn't it?" It was a statement rather than a question. Rob, always calmer than his friend, nodded in agreement but was already thinking ahead. "So, when will they make their next move, and what will it be?"

Velma shrugged her shoulders. "My guess is they will make their move any time soon. What it will be depends on local conditions, but remember, we are talking about Africa here." She shot a quick glance at Rob to see his reaction to her last remark, but Rob knew what she meant. "If I understand you correctly, you believe that Diaby could be in grave danger." Velma agreed. "If you want to save him, he needs to have his card marked as soon as possible.

In my opinion, there is no time to lose."

The audience seemed over, and the men rose from their chairs. They thanked Velma for her input and Dottie for her hospitality. They now had a clear idea about what was happening in Kwandia and could not wait to return to their hotel.

*******************************************

It was lunchtime when they returned to their room, but before they made their way along to the restaurant, Rob had two tasks to complete and withdrew his laptop from its case. Firstly, he wanted to get back to London as soon as possible and the late night flight on British Airways to Heathrow would be ideal. He was not overly disappointed to find that the only seats available were in business class, so he promptly booked them. Travelling through the night cramped up in economy seats did not appeal to him. Declan shrugged his shoulders when he was told but had to accept the situation. However, an afterthought struck him, and he enquired why Rob had not tried to book on one of the American airlines. "I suppose they are not 'British' enough for you?"

The comment made by Velma obviously still rankled with him, and Rob could not resist adding further fuel to the fire. "You do realise she was talking geographically rather than politically, of course." Declan looked puzzled. "What are you talking about?" Rob laughed. "Well, the British

Isles is a geographical term that includes the whole of Ireland, so under that definition, you could be described as a 'Brit' whereas Great Britain is a political definition that excludes Ireland, so you are definitely not British."

Declan was not to be beaten. "And you honestly think she knows that. Most Americans couldn't find Ireland on a map?" He could not resist a further dig at Rob. "Amazing what a Cambridge education can do for you."

Quick as a flash, Rob came back. "You mean the same education as you had?" reminding his friend where they had met, but before Declan could respond, he added, "As a matter of fact, it was something I learnt whilst gaining UK citizenship." Declan acknowledged defeat. "Very commendable," was all he could say.

Rob then turned his attention to his second task.

He needed to get a message to Simon Fellowes as soon as possible. There were two problems to overcome. Firstly, maintaining secrecy as Simon's only access to the internet was by using a computer in his office and available to all the staff. Secondly, the unreliability of the local internet connection in Kwandia. He could do nothing about the latter, but during Simon's visit to the UK, they had arranged a coded communication protocol, which they hoped would ensure confidentiality. It would take more time, but they could not risk the message getting into the wrong hands.

He entered the email address he had been given and rather laboriously typed out the words using only one finger on each hand. Declan, who, as a journalist, was rather more proficient on a keyboard, looked on in amusement. Over Rob's shoulder, he read the missive, which was short and sweet. 'This is a private message for Simon Fellowes. I have urgent information regarding the health of your son Julian. Please acknowledge this message and let me know ASAP whether you can stand by your computer to receive such information at 11 am tomorrow. Regards, Doctor Robson Ford.'

Declan nodded his approval. "Let us hope he receives it. What time is it there?"

Rob had done his homework. "It is about ten past six in the evening. They are five hours ahead of us. Even if he doesn't pick it up today, he should see it first thing in the morning. There is no time difference with the UK, and by then, we can be back in my surgery ready to send part two."

Declan grinned. "Very impressive, young Robbie. Let us hope our plane is not delayed."

# Chapter 21 - Explosion

Despite the comfort of business class and the few hours of sleep they had managed, both men felt slightly weary when they met up in Rob's surgery at ten thirty the following morning. Simon Fellowes had acknowledged the first message and would be standing by at eleven o'clock. Aided by coffees supplied by Mary, they began to draft the message. This time, Declan was at the keyboard whilst Rob dictated the wording. They wanted to make it as short as possible but with enough information so that Simon would know what he had to do.

After some edits and corrections, Declan pulled up the final version on the screen. With Rob's approval, he cut and pasted the words into the draft folder of the email account.

> *'The vaccine confers no medical benefit as it is no more than a weak saline solution. However, it does contain a miniature microchip, which we believe will form the basis of an ID project and possible introduction of digital currency. This is clearly being carried out without the knowledge and consent of the recipients, so we believe the vaccine programme should be ceased immediately. We also think that those behind the project are likely negotiating with a local source (Kyabou?) to obtain the mineral rights for the lithium ore recently discovered in the country. If President Diaby is not fully*

*aware of this information, it would suggest his position may be under threat, and he should be made aware of the facts as soon as possible.'*

At precisely 11 o'clock, they received a message from Simon saying he was ready. Declan pressed the 'send' button on their own message. After a few minutes, Simon replied.

*'Message received and understood. I am shocked by the contents. Luckily, I am attending a cocktail party at Diaby's official residence this evening, so I will have a chance to discuss your findings with him. I am sure he knows nothing of either of these projects. I shall need to tread carefully.'*

There was little more the men could do now except wait for news. It could be some time before Simon would be able to contact them again. The parting shot in Simon's email reminded them that it was not only the President who was in danger. Anyone, such as Simon, who had this information, was at risk. It all depended now on the President's reaction.

***********************************

When no news came for several days, Rob and Declan began to get impatient. At the very least, Rob had expected a message from Simon informing him of how the President had reacted to the news.

He wasn't sure what to make of the silence. Then, one afternoon, the telephone rang, and Mary put through a call from Kate Fellowes. She explained to Rob that Simon's meeting with the President had caused 'the balloon to go up', which is how she phrased it. Simon had been advised to leave the country as quickly as possible and was due home in two days' time. He had told her to watch the news bulletins as something was about to happen, but he had given no further information. Rob expressed his concern for Simon and hoped he would soon be back safe and sound.

In the meantime, he would continue to scan the news apps on his mobile phone. He had also taken to walking up to Bond Street station from the surgery during his lunch break to pick up the early edition of the Evening Standard. It was the very day after Kate's call that he spotted a headline in that newspaper tucked away halfway down the page in the section covering world news. The People's Republic of Kwandia did not rate that high in the league table of international affairs, and it was not a lengthy report. Even so, he was shocked by the headline.

### 'Kwandian minister killed by car bomb'

Reading further, the report referred to the death of Kwandia's Minister of Finance, Nouha Kyabou, in a car bomb attack in the northern part of the country where he was visiting the new wing of a hospital. An aide and the driver of his car were also killed. In announcing this tragedy, President Diaby blamed an extremist group known to be active in this area. He went on to praise Kyabou as a clever and talented Minister whose qualities will be sorely missed in Government. He promised to hunt down those responsible.

The last sentence brought a rueful smile to Rob's face. At least they now knew that Velma's assessment of the situation was vindicated, and they also now understood that Diaby was a ruthless operator. He had wasted no time in removing any threat to his presidency.

It was a fact brought home to him when Simon Fellowes paid a visit to his surgery a few days later. Simon described the situation in Kwandia as 'fragile'. Despite the fact that it was Simon who had tipped off his friend Diaby and probably saved his life, the President warned him that no one could feel safe. In theory, he controlled the militia, but once news had leaked out about the bogus vaccine, any Westerner could become a target. Simon was particularly despondent. "Actually, it is even worse than that. Before I left, I saw planeloads of Chinese arriving, both civilians and military. Word has it that Diaby has made a deal with them granting lithium mineral rights, and they have also agreed to fund some of the charitable projects, including my own. I don't suppose I shall ever go back there."

Rob expressed his sympathy and, in response to Simon's enquiry, began to fill him in on the trail of discovery that he and Declan had followed. He described the tests that were carried out on the vaccine and their research into what the tiny microchips might be used for. Simon's face clouded over when he mentioned the death of Professor Lewis and his own suspicions.

Simon jumped in at this point. "Why didn't you contact me immediately when you found out about the vaccine?"

Rob understood his point and tried to explain. "We did consider it, but at that stage, we only had half a story. Furthermore, we had no idea who knew what in Kwandia. We couldn't be absolutely sure that Diaby wasn't also backing the vaccine project. Such knowledge could have put you in grave danger. It was only after we visited America that we were able to learn more about the Doorstep Foundation and put all the pieces together."

Simon seemed satisfied with this explanation but was also astonished to learn they had travelled to America on his behalf. Rob accepted the plaudit gracefully but knew that, in reality, their motivation had a loftier aim than simply protecting Simon. He described their visit to Velma Stanway and what they had learned about Jim Doors and the Doorstep Foundation. "It put the whole thing into context, and we realised that this was a plot to overthrow Diaby so that the Americans could install their puppet Kyabou and grab the rights to the lithium mining. We are still not entirely sure of the ultimate purpose behind the vaccination project, but we believe it to be a major ID experiment using the citizens of Kwandia as guinea pigs with a possible follow-up of introducing a digital currency in the country. That would give the Americans effective control."

Simon shook his head in amazement. "So, it becomes like a colony in all but name." Rob agreed. "That is a good way of putting it."

# Chapter 22 - Escape

Oumou Kyabou knew they would come for her even though she genuinely knew nothing of her husband's political plots and knew no more about the vaccine project than the average citizen of Kwandia. She needed to get away and get away fast.

She was sitting in her cousin's living room next to two large suitcases, waiting for her cousin's husband to come round to the front of the house with a car to take her to the airport. Unusually for her, she was wearing the full niqab, the most concealing form of dress for Muslim women. Though the population was predominantly Muslim, Kwandia was relaxed about dress codes in day-to-day life, and like most modern young women, Oumou only wore a burka or niqab when visiting the mosque or on special religious occasions. However, there were times when such a cover-up came in useful. This was one of those times.

In addition to the suitcases, she was also taking the large (and expensive) designer handbag she had bought on her recent visit to Paris. While waiting, she withdrew the white envelope her husband had entrusted to her care, which was only to be opened in the event of his untimely death. She had already opened it that morning but wanted to study it again and memorise as much of its contents as she could.

She emptied the envelope onto a side table and

took each item in turn. There were two sheets of closely typed A4 paper. One was an official-looking document in German, which she managed to discern was his last will and testament. Fortunately, the reverse side contained a complete transcript in French, which allowed her to understand its key features. Basically, he had left all his worldly possessions to her, but most importantly, she was to inherit his position as director of the Citizens of Kwandia Trust and as sole signatory of its Swiss bank account.

The other sheet of paper contained a list of instructions numbered from one to twenty. She wiped away a small tear as she thought of her husband composing this list. He was always a 'belt and braces' man, and the remarkable degree of detail in these instructions reflected that. As did another slightly smaller sheet of paper, which was an official death certificate for himself. Who else would have thought of that? Instruction number one required her to enter the date and cause of death and then take several copies. He had thought of everything.

Inside the large white envelope was also a smaller brown envelope, which was firmly sealed. She slit it open and discovered bank documents and cards relating to two Swiss bank accounts. There were statements for each account, and her eyes nearly popped out of her head when she saw the balances on each account, particularly that in the name of the Citizens of Kwandia Trust. She picked up the list of instructions and scanned down to those referring to the bank accounts. Her heart missed a beat. She could scarcely contain her excitement.

The envelope contained two other items, and she took them out and stared at them. Firstly, an exceedingly good fake French passport in the name of Yasmin Chebel. Her photograph stared back at her. Secondly, a French identity card with the same name and with a similar photograph. The two documents brought home to her that this was probably the last day she would spend in the country of her birth and that not only would her life now be spent elsewhere, but she would also assume a new identity. But first, she had to escape from her country, and the French documents were the key to getting her through border controls at Diaby International Airport.

She had also to prepare herself for a long journey. There were at least three stops and possibly three changes of plane. She wasn't sure. The instructions did not specify.

In any event, she got away with no difficulty, and when she eventually arrived in Zurich, she went straight to the information desk at the airport and requested them to book her into one of the city's five-star hotels. They advised the Baur au Lac hotel, which was not only centrally situated but overlooked Lake Zurich as the name implied and had a view of the Alps in the background. Once established in her luxurious room, she dumped her niqab in the wardrobe and changed into her designer top and jeans. Following the instructions, her next action was to call Dr Kraft. After offering his condolences, he quickly got down to business and arranged to collect her the following morning. He would make the necessary arrangements with Herr Lerner at the bank in Zug.

That evening, she referred back to her list of instructions. In preparation for the morning, she switched her Kwandian passport back to her handbag and began thinking about what she should wear. Proving her identity was crucial to the exercise, and although she had the necessary documentation for that, she wondered what they would expect and whether she should revert to the niqab. After tossing the idea about in her head, she decided that formal business attire, such as her smart trouser suit would be preferable. She wanted them to understand that they were dealing with a powerful woman here and not think they could treat her like an uneducated member of the harem.

***********************************

The following morning, Dr Kraft arrived promptly in his white BMW. En route to Zug, he explained to Oumou that they would first call in at his office to deal with the formalities relating to the Citizens' Trust. She was asked whether they should close it down. She pretended to consider the matter, but she knew the answer. One of the instructions was quite clear. Move all the money from the Trust's bank account into the numbered account, which was her inheritance, and then wind up the Trust. She informed Dr Kraft accordingly, who nodded his understanding. "Of course." He then telephoned Herr Lerner from the car and gave him some brief instructions in German.

The formalities in Dr Kraft's office did not take long, and Oumou was soon comfortably settled in Herr Lerner's office in the bank, partaking of one of his excellent pastries, which she felt she needed to make up for the breakfast she had skipped earlier. She was impressed with the efficiency of the Swiss as the banker handed her a small folder containing all the necessary documents and bank cards to manage her account. It all seemed so easy.

Back at her hotel, she was able to relax and began to ponder her next move. She would check out in the morning and take a flight from Zurich to Nice in France. While placing her French passport in her handbag, she realised that she needed to start planning for more than just the immediate future; she needed to plan for the rest of her life. Oumou Kyabou had disappeared from the face of the earth. She was now Yasmin Chebel. She would find a pleasant apartment in Nice. Perhaps she might look for a job; after all, she had a medical degree from the Sorbonne in Paris. But then she smiled to herself. There was no hurry; ten million dollars in the bank should keep her going comfortably for as long as she wanted.

# Chapter 23 - The Foreign Office

At the same time that Oumou met her Swiss lawyer and banker, another meeting took place in a small conference room in the Foreign and Commonwealth Office at King Charles Street in London. In truth, the word 'meeting' was hardly an appropriate description of what was happening. It was far from the convivial and businesslike affair in Zug, more like a showdown.

On one side of the table stood Sir Thomas Daltrey flanked by three aides, two men and a woman, sitting on either side of him. Opposite were seated two men who, it transpired, were from the middle management ranks of MI6, the secret service arm within the Foreign Office. Sir Thomas was in full rant mode, and the two men bowed their heads in an effort to avoid looking at him. It was rare for the senior diplomat to lose his cool, but his aides knew he could resort to 'industrial language' when the occasion demanded. However, this was something else, and the aides exchanged embarrassed glances and shifted somewhat uneasily in their seats as their boss's diatribe descended further until it became little more than a string of obscenities and abuse.

"You fucking morons! What the fuck did you think you were doing?" The men said nothing. "Did you arseholes not see fit to report your activities up the line? You fucking idiots have not only destroyed years of painstaking diplomacy, but you have gifted a loyal ally straight into the arms of the fucking Chinese. Was that your plan?"

Finally, one of the men attempted to speak. "No sir, quite the contrary. We were simply helping the Americans and were sworn to secrecy." His words did nothing to placate Sir Thomas. "I bet you bloody well were!"

For all his bluster, Sir Thomas had now run out of steam. Nothing else was to be said, and the two men left the room. He sat down in his chair and looked at his team. "Fucking disaster" was his final summing up.

**\*\*\*\*\*\*\*\*\*\*\*\*\*\*\*\*\*\*\*\*\*\*\*\*\*\*\*\*\*\*\*\*\*\*\***

That evening, when Rob arrived home after a routine day at the surgery, he found his wife talking on the telephone to her father. She passed the phone to him before he could even sit down. "He wants to talk to you."

He sat down and listened to the cultured tones of Sir Richard Prentice, who got straight to the point, "I assume you have seen the news relating to Kwandia." Rob confirmed that he had, and Sir Richard continued. "I spoke to my contact at the Foreign Office earlier and thought you might like an update."

He didn't wait for a reply but carried on. "You

were right to be suspicious of the vaccine. The whole project was a complete fake set-up by the Americans with no medical benefit whatsoever. It seems that their real aim was to remove the President and install their own puppet in his place. Something to do with acquiring some valuable mineral rights before the Chinese could get their hands on them. Unfortunately for them, someone tipped off the President and the whole thing blew up in their faces, you could say literally."

Rob thanked his father-in-law for the information, but Sir Richard hadn't finished. He gave a slight cough before speaking and then sounded rather embarrassed. "I am afraid it was not my old Department's finest hour. It seems that they had two sections working in opposite directions."

"Oh dear," Rob tried to sound sympathetic.

"Regrettably, the outcome was the worst of both worlds. The British are no longer welcome in Kwandia, and to cap it all, the Chinese will walk off with the mineral rights."

Rob could think of no adequate response, and even though the word disastrous hovered on his lips, he said nothing. Sir Richard was ever the diplomat and ended the conversation with one of his masterly understatements. "All in all, it was less than satisfactory."

Having put the phone down, he stretched out his

long legs on their smart, Italian leather sofa, first kicking off his shoes to avoid a reprimand from Alice. His adventure was now over, and in theory, he could relax, but for reasons he couldn't quite place, he still felt a sense of unease, and his mind was not at rest. He had always admired the smooth diplomatic skills of his father-in-law, but on this occasion, his final summing up did not ease his frame of mind. If anything, it had the opposite effect.

After all, in the past few weeks, he had been physically beaten up on his own doorstep, a retired professor had been murdered, and three people had been blown to pieces by a car bomb. Not only that, but almost the entire population of a small African country had been injected with a fake vaccine. "Less than satisfactory" seemed an inadequate description, and more than that revealed a certain cold-heartedness which he had never sensed before. It did nothing to lighten his mood or prevent his mind from wandering into a reflective consideration of his life to date.

He was so focused on his goals that he had never given much thought to the broader implications of the knowledge being drummed into him or the values he was absorbing.

His musing took him back to his start in life as a small boy in a Zambian village. His mother instilled in him a love of all things British, and good old Doctor Fiesta inspired his medical ambition. When he stopped to think about it, he realised his progress to his position today had been amazingly smooth and rapid. He accepted that some luck and the encouragement of others had contributed to this, but he understood that his own God-given talent and inner drive must have played a role in his achievements. He readily took the Hippocratic Oath, swearing to uphold a number of professional ethical standards, and in acquiring UK citizenship, he had not only sworn allegiance to the Crown but also promised to respect the rights, freedoms and laws of the UK. Whilst he saw these as necessary rites of passage, he had never thought to question the values they espoused and just assumed he was joining a 'club' of like-minded people.

Now married to a diplomat's daughter and with a thriving medical practice in the prestigious location of Harley Street, he recognised that he had become part of the 'Establishment'. But his recent experiences had caused him to question beliefs he had always taken for granted or never really thought about. He had found the memorial gathering for Professor Lewis and their subsequent meetings with the American lawyer and Velma Stanway profoundly disturbing. His eyes had been opened to another side of life, and he even saw his friend Declan in a new light. As an Irishman, Declan had never shared his mother's reverence 'for all things British'. He had always laughed off his friend's occasional sardonic comment about the British in the past, but his perspective had now changed.

He was so lost in his reverie that he hardly noticed Alice sitting down and squeezing in beside him. She observed his contemplative mood and began to stroke his head fondly. "After all the excitement, wasn't it good to get back to the same old routine?" He looked up and nodded his agreement, planting a big kiss on her forehead. Yes, he was happy to return to the familiar, but Alice had used the word 'same'. He sat back in the chair and sighed. Doctor Robson Ford realised that nothing in his life would ever be quite the same again.

The End

# Epilogue

The summers in Texas are hot. In the cavernous living room of Jim Doors' luxury ranch house, the flames of the artificial gas fire had long since given way to the soft background humming of the aircon, which on this day had been set so that the temperature in the room was pleasantly mild, neither too hot nor too cold.

The two men were in their usual chairs, but the thin lips of Albin Millard were pursed in an ill-tempered fashion, which gave the Cadaver's face an even more disagreeable expression than usual. "So, it was a complete fuck-up then."

The Shark leant forward in the chair facing him and sipped his twelve-year-old bourbon. After savouring the taste, his face broke into a broad grin, although it was not a grin of amusement but perhaps more of a grimace. Either way, his facial expression was much the same, and the white teeth he was renowned for glinted in the sunshine. The effect was threatening rather than benign, and even the Cadaver felt a cold chill run down his spine. "Yeah, I guess 'fuck-up' is the right word for it."

"Was it Glik?"

The Shark was quick to reply. "No, I don't think we can blame him. It was just a bit of bad luck. They gave the vaccine to some 'limey' kid who was out there visiting his dad, and an interfering medic from London followed it up."

The Cadaver nodded as if he understood, but his concern was focused elsewhere. "So, what about our little investment?"

Jim Doors sighed and shrugged his broad shoulders. "Gone, I'm afraid."

"Gone?" The Cadaver could not believe his ears. "What d'yer mean, gone?"

"I got Glik to contact the bank. The Trust has been closed, and the bank account cleaned out."

Albin Millard was not pleased. "That was ten million bucks down the tubes."

Another shrug of the shoulders from the Shark. "Well, you know the old saying. You have to speculate to accumulate. But when you speculate, you sometimes lose, and this time, we lost. But ten million is not so heavy in the grand scheme of things."

His words did nothing to placate the Cadaver. For men used to dealing in billions, the Shark's comments were true, but Albin had come up the hard way, and his reputation as a financial wizard was earned by taking care of every nickel and dime. Waste was not part of his vocabulary.

The Shark's teeth reappeared as his face broke into a broad smile. "It has not been all waste, Al. We may well be able to use the vaccine production facility of ME Chemicals in the not-too-distant future. I heard some of the guys have been registering vaccine patents as fast as they can find them."

Albin took an interest in all developments in the medical world not only from an investment point of view but also an obsession with his personal health. "Yeah, I know. I have a piece of three of them."

Knowing his friend, Jim Doors was not entirely surprised. "Sounds like you're ahead of me Al, so what's the angle?"

The Cadaver's face relaxed a little from his previous disgruntled expression and the thin lips almost formed themselves into a smile as he weighed up how best to explain 'the angle' as the Shark had put it. "Well, you need to appreciate a bit of background, some of it scientific, but I'll try and keep it as simple as I can."

"I'd appreciate that." Once again, the teeth became visible, but Albin could not tell whether his friend was smiling from amusement or indulging him. Nevertheless, he carried on. "Do you know what 'gain-of-function' research is?" The Shark shook his head, and the teeth receded into his jawline. "Well, 'gain-of-function' is a controversial form of research which takes a pathogen such as a virus or a germ and mutates it, so it develops new properties.

Often, the mutations are more transmissible than the original and potentially deadly to humans, which is why such research can only be carried out in level 4 laboratories, that is to say, those having the highest level of biosafety. Even so, leaks can occur, and after an incident three years ago at one of these labs in our country where they were working on a particular virus, Obama prohibited all such 'gain-of-function research.

Jim Doors said nothing but continued to wait for the punch line.

"Instead of ceasing the research, they moved it to the Institute of Virology located in China at some place called Wuhan, but the Americans continued to provide funds from taxpayers' money for the project."

Jim was intrigued. "So, what's the play?"

"Well, Chinese security is not considered up to American standards, and a lot of scientists believe it is only a matter of time before one of these nasty viruses escapes into the world. So, all the new vaccine patents tend to be concentrated in one area, that is to say, respiratory infections. When an 'incident' occurs, the vaccine investors will lean heavily on the world's health authorities to declare a pandemic and speed up the development of the appropriate vaccines in response."

The Shark's teeth reappeared in a broad grin. He

was not interested in the science, but his predatory instincts were now on full alert. Unlike his namesake in the ocean, this particular shark was not sniffing blood and the prospect of a good meal. Instead, his olfactory sense was savouring a different smell, the sweet smell of 'dollars', millions of them. He sat bolt upright in his chair and looked his friend in the eye. "A pandemic, eh? Bring it on!"

*'You know when that shark bites with his teeth, babe*
*Scarlet billows start to spread.'*
Mack the Knife

# Authors Note

The characters in this book are entirely fictitious, and any resemblance to persons living or dead would be coincidental.

The African state of Kwandia is also imaginary and does not exist. Most other locations are real enough, but corporations such as Hague Chemicals, ME Chemicals, etc, are made up. Likewise, there is no such organisation as MAGIC, although there are several institutions with global health objectives.

The book refers to a 'Verein', a type of Swiss Trust used as a form of the legal constitution by many well-known international associations.

Printed in Great Britain
by Amazon

62032595R00117